Once Upon a Winter

Don't miss the place where
the adventures began!

ICE CREAM SUMMER

Or the adventures to come!

A FALL FOR FRIENDSHIP

· AN ORCHARD NOVEL ·

Once Upon a Winter

By Megan Atwood

Illustrated by Natalie Andrewson

ALADDIN

New York   London   Toronto   Sydney   New Delhi

ALADDIN

An imprint of Simon & Schuster Children's Publishing Division
1230 Avenue of the Americas, New York, New York 10020
First Aladdin hardcover edition December 2017
Text copyright © 2017 by Simon & Schuster, Inc.
Illustrations copyright © 2017 by Natalie Andrewson
All rights reserved, including the right of reproduction in whole or in part in any form.
ALADDIN and related logo are registered trademarks of Simon & Schuster, Inc.
For information about special discounts for bulk purchases, please contact Simon & Schuster Special Sales at 1-866-506-1949 or business@simonandschuster.com.
The Simon & Schuster Speakers Bureau can bring authors to your live event. For more information or to book an event contact the Simon & Schuster Speakers Bureau at 1-866-248-3049 or visit our website at www.simonspeakers.com.
Book designed by Laura Lyn DiSiena
The illustrations for this book were rendered digitally.
The text of this book was set in Baskerville.
Manufactured in the United States of America 1117 FFG
10 9 8 7 6 5 4 3 2 1
Library of Congress Cataloging-in-Publication Data
Names: Atwood, Megan, author. | Andrewson, Natalie, illustrator.
Title: Once upon a winter / by Megan Atwood ; illustrated by Natalie Andrewson
Description: First Aladdin hardcover edition. | New York : Aladdin, 2017. |
Series: An Orchard novel ; 2 | Summary: Feeling out of sorts with his twin sister, Olive, and their friends Lizzie and Sarah, Peter is drawn to new student Kai, but soon discovers that Kai is not very nice.
Identifiers: LCCN 2017033103 (print) | LCCN 2017044603 (eBook) |
ISBN 9781481490504 (eBook) | ISBN 9781481490498 (hardcover)
Subjects: | CYAC: Friendship—Fiction. | Conduct of life—Fiction. |
Twins—Fiction. | Brothers and sisters—Fiction. | Schools—Fiction. |
Apples—Fiction. | Orchards—Fiction. | New England—Fiction.
Classification: LCC PZ7.A8952 (eBook) | LCC PZ7.A8952 Op 2017 (print) |
DDC [Fic]—dc23
LC record available at https://lccn.loc.gov/2017033103

To my Minnesota kidlit family—

don't forget me. I adore you all.

CHAPTER 1

Magic Is in the Air

Peter watched the snow come down, swirling and white, like a magic spell come to life, and listened to the chaos behind him. His house was packed, like normal on game night. Most of the time he didn't mind. And his dads loved hosting. But today the world seemed a little off. He rolled his shoulders and tried to shake the feeling.

"Are you here with us, Peter?" a voice said near

his ear. His twin, Olive, climbed up next to him in the window seat. Her eyes looked worried— she'd started having a tiny little crease on her forehead every time she talked to him lately. She knew something was wrong. There *was* something wrong, but Peter wasn't exactly sure he could put words around it. Maybe he felt sad because he missed his friends in Boston. Or because every time he talked, someone interrupted him. Or because he'd felt beside the point ever since they'd moved to New Amity. And that their new best friends, Sarah and Lizzie, were really just Olive's new best friends.

Maybe he felt sad because it seemed like he was from a different world and didn't belong here.

Mostly, he felt a big ball of emotions that he

didn't know what to do with. So the snow seemed simpler at the moment. Plus, the way it sparkled under the streetlight made it look like it was winking at him.

With some effort, he dragged his gaze away from the snow and said, "I'm here." He couldn't think of anything else to say so he just looked at Olive.

Olive huffed. "Of course you're here. I mean are you going to come hang out? We're getting ready to play charades. Kids against the grown-ups—you know we'll win!" She smiled at him, and he couldn't help but smile back.

He loved playing with Olive, especially when they played guessing games. Olive and Peter each always knew what the other one was thinking—they had since birth. He stood up and tried to shake off his mood. "I'm definitely in." Olive grinned and stood up.

His dad John said, "Uh-oh. I think we're in trouble," when Peter and Olive walked into the living room. David, his other dad, said almost at the same time, "Let's not make any bets, okay?" Peter looked at the Garrisons. Tabitha and Albert Garrison owned the oldest apple orchard in New England. When Peter and Olive had first moved to the town, they'd met the Garrisons' daughter Lizzie, who was their age. And Sarah was Lizzie's best friend. The four of them had been inseparable ever since.

The Garrisons had another, older daughter named Gloria. She was a little . . . weird. But Peter liked how she had committed herself to becoming an actress. Even if it was a little annoying.

"Why can't we make bets?" Sarah asked, a huge whipped-cream mustache on her upper lip. She licked it off and took another big drink of her hot chocolate. She and Lizzie sat together in one of the overstuffed antique chairs Peter's dad David had gotten. The house they were renting was a large Queen Anne, and David had decided the whole house would be decorated in different periods of antiques.

Lizzie was trying to catch a marshmallow in her hot chocolate with her tongue. "Do we normally make bets?" she asked, confused for a second. But she caught the marshmallow and didn't seem to care about the answer. She smiled at Peter when he joined them. Lizzie and Peter were the most alike. Even though Olive and he were twins, they had very different personalities. But

Lizzie and Peter were both quiet and were okay if Sarah and Olive took charge. And they always did. Sometimes at the same time.

"Okay," said Tabitha, "let's let the kids go first." She snuggled into Albert, her husband, on the antique settee. Peter's dads also sat back on the huge velvet davenport and snuggled in, and Peter noticed that Sheriff Hadley and Ms. Shirvani also sat pretty close together at the other end. He glanced at Sarah—did she know her mom and the sheriff seemed to be . . . well, closer than most friends?

Sarah and Olive said at the same time, "I'll go first." But then Gloria swept in and said, "All right, darling babies. I shall show you how one *inhabits* a role."

She grabbed a piece of paper before anyone

could say anything. "Please do start the timer," Gloria said, looking down her nose at the adults. Gloria was the only kid Peter knew who could do that and make it look convincing.

John turned the hourglass timer over, and Gloria looked at the piece of paper with the charades word on it. She set the paper down, closed her eyes, and whispered, "Acting!" to herself. Then she opened her eyes again and widened them. She let out a huge roar and made her arms beat up and down like wings.

"A bat!" said Lizzie.

"A vulture!" said Olive.

"A flying lion?" said Sarah.

Peter didn't say anything. He had no idea what it could possibly be. Gloria made her mouth into an O and then moved her head back

7

and forth, like she was blowing on everyone.

It reminded him of something . . .

His new video game, *Elf Mirror*! There was a dragon in there that made exactly those movements. He had just gotten the game a few days ago and already he'd become obsessed with it. In fact, it was hard for him to sit and play charades with everyone when *Elf Mirror* sat in his room. But here he was, and he knew what Gloria was acting out.

"A dragon," he said quietly.

"A hose!" Olive yelled.

"Jack Frost!" Lizzie said. Everyone looked at her, and she shrank back. "What? Mom and I are reading about winter lore at night." Tabitha grinned and winked at her, but Gloria stamped her foot in frustration.

"A flying lion with bad breath?" Sarah guessed.

Lizzie and Olive giggled, and Peter snickered too.

"A dragon," he said, but the girls had started shouting again and no one heard him.

"Time!" his dad said, holding up the hourglass.

Gloria huffed. "What would I expect from *babies*? I was a dragon, clearly." She flounced off to another antique chair and plopped down. Peter saw his dad cringe at how hard Gloria sat in the chair.

"I said that," Peter said, but everyone had started talking again and the grown-ups were taking their turn.

Maybe he wasn't really there after all.

When it was the kids' turn again, Olive turned to Peter. "Why don't you go?" He knew she was saying that so they could easily get a point. He nodded and stood up.

As he grabbed the paper with the word, his dad John said, "Ready?" He flipped over the hourglass timer just as Peter flipped over the paper.

His word was "hero."

That was a hard one. He took a second to think about how he would perform his charade. The room was quiet, making him nervous. He wasn't a fan of having all the attention. It made him tongue-tied.

But he knew how to do this. Easy.

Looking at Olive, he pointed to Gloria. Olive said, "Acting?"

Peter shook his head. He mimicked the actions Gloria had done. Lizzie said, "Dragon?"

He nodded. He was more than a little surprised that Olive hadn't gotten that but Lizzie had. Still, he had no time to think about it.

Sarah yelled, "Dragon Gloria!" Everyone looked at her, and Gloria rolled her eyes.

Peter mimicked riding a horse and holding a spear. He didn't like horses, but he didn't mind riding a fake one. Olive guessed, "Horse!" and Peter grinned. Now they were in sync. When he mimed thrusting the spear at Gloria and then getting off his horse and celebrating, Olive guessed, "Olympic medalist!"

He stopped to furrow his eyebrows at her. How could that possibly be her guess? Sarah guessed, "Party dragon Gloria!" and Lizzie said, "Happy horse rider?"

These were not charades terms. Peter was pretty sure no one had ever gotten the charades phrase "happy horse rider." He looked at Olive with wide eyes, trying to will her into understanding him. He said in his mind, over and over, "Hero, hero, hero."

Olive guessed, "Dragon rider?"

"Time!" said John. Peter's heart sank.

Not so much because they'd missed a point. But the big ball of lonely seemed to be back. He shrugged and avoided Olive's eyes as he sat down. For the rest of the game, he barely participated. He looked out at the snow swirling around outside, wishing he was in it. It really did look magical. Like the world had turned into something different in front of his very eyes.

After the game—which the kids lost handily— the whole crew grabbed more cider or hot chocolate and sat down around the fire again. Everyone seemed to cozy up to everyone else. Lizzie, Sarah, and Olive sat close, whispering to each other and giggling every once in a while. Peter couldn't take his eyes off the snow.

Tabitha and Albert started talking about the holiday season at the orchard. "This time between Thanksgiving and the solstice is probably our biggest season. That and the beginning of fall. If you want to help out at the orchard and make some money, Peter and Olive, we'd love to have you!"

Peter turned his attention to the conversation. Olive pushed her glasses up her nose and beamed. Her answer was definitely yes. But Peter wanted to know more.

"What kind of help?" he asked, turning away from the window.

"Well, we give sleigh rides and tours—we'd love help with those. There's a snowperson-making contest where we need people to help with setup, a baked goods sale where we need help advertising and organizing . . . we could use help decorating in general for the season! We need to put up our giant Christmas tree and the huge menorah. Our solstice celebration brings a ton of people in. Would you be interested?" Tabitha smiled warmly.

"I'm in!" Sarah said, which surprised no one.

Lizzie shrugged. "I sort of have to." Tabitha winked at her.

Olive said, "Can I, Dads?"

Peter noticed she didn't say "we."

David beamed. "Of course! That sounds just lovely. Thank you, Tabitha and Albert. Peter, are you interested?"

John piped up. "I think that would be a really good idea. Peter, I think you should help with the sleigh rides." He looked meaningfully at Peter.

Peter frowned. He was not a fan of horses; they scared him, which was why his dad was trying to get him to agree. Years ago he'd gone to horseback-riding camp and had gotten bucked off a horse. He had loved camp until then and had learned all sorts of things. But the lesson he'd learned more than anything was that horses were mean.

He wanted to help at the orchard—he really did. The thought of his friends getting to do something together without him made a pang shoot through him. Suddenly, out of nowhere, Peter missed his friends in Boston more than he had since his family had moved to New Amity. He hadn't had a ton of friends, but he'd had a few. They were all boys, and it was different to hang around with them, but he'd loved it. Just like he used to love hanging around with Sarah and Lizzie. And, he realized with another pang, Olive. Something had changed between him and Olive, and he didn't know what.

"Okay, I can help," he finally said. Maybe this would make things better. Maybe he'd feel like he had close friends again.

And maybe his dad was right: perhaps it was time to stop being afraid of horses. After all, he was in middle school already. It wasn't like he was a kid anymore. He didn't have to like horses, but he should at least stop being afraid of them.

He swallowed. "I'll help with the sleigh rides, too."

Olive said, "I'll help *with* you."

Something about that irritated Peter. It would

have been nice if she'd asked him if he wanted her to help. Being twins, siblings, and best friends since birth didn't mean Peter couldn't do things on his own.

Albert said, "Peter and Olive, you'll love winter at the orchard. Something about the snow makes everything feel magical. Like anything can happen."

"It's like a whole different world," Lizzie said, her eyes shining.

A small tendril of hope broke through Peter's gloominess. They'd said the exact words he'd been thinking. This had to be a sign. He hoped this new world would be one where he didn't feel quite so alone and unheard.

CHAPTER 2
Through the Wardrobe

"PETER!" his dad David's voice traveled upstairs and cut through the music playing on *Elf Mirror*. Peter knew this meant he was close to getting in trouble, but he had almost found the right spell to enter the world where the dragon lived. If he could just . . .

The TV turned off and his dad stood in front of him. "Peter Thomas Wu, I have been calling you for ten minutes. You're going to be late for school! And you didn't even have breakfast."

David wore his long apron, which meant he'd be welding today.

Peter groaned and rolled his eyes. He put down the controller and got up, barely looking at his dad.

David moved closer to him. "Honey, are you okay? You just haven't been yourself lately."

Peter shrugged on his backpack and turned around. He put on a smile. "I'm fine."

His dad looked him in the eyes for a few more seconds and then said, "Well, the girls are waiting for you downstairs. Grab a granola bar on your way out, and don't forget your lunch!" His dad squeezed his shoulder, and Peter walked down the stairs. His dad yelled after him, "I think Olive took the phone, honey!"

Olive and Peter shared a cell phone, each getting to have it on alternate days. Peter never really paid attention to it anymore. None of his Boston friends texted him much, and most of the texts were from Sarah and Lizzie to Olive.

"Took ya long enough!" Sarah said cheerfully when he joined the group. They all walked to school together when the weather was good enough. The walk was pretty far, but all the adults thought it was a good idea for them to get fresh air and exercise. Olive shot him an irritated look—if they were late and it was Peter's fault, she would be mad for hours. Lizzie looked at him and said, "Hey, Peter. Hope you're doing okay."

Peter said, "I was playing *Elf Mirror*," and he saw Olive roll her eyes.

For some reason, he felt like he needed to

explain to her. The game meant a lot to him right now. When he played it, he felt like he belonged somewhere. "It's a really good game, Olive. There's this mirror, and on the other side of it, there's a land that needs a hero. There's a dragon that is menacing the whole world, and once you go through the mirror, you have to find all these—"

"It's not real life, Peter. In real life, we have to get to school on time," Olive said, walking a little faster. Lizzie and Sarah exchanged a look. Sarah walked faster to catch up with Olive, and Lizzie hung back with Peter.

After a second, Lizzie said, "The game sounds fun."

Peter melted just a little. He could always count on Lizzie to make him feel better. He didn't know why Olive was SO mad at him. But he was most surprised to find out: it didn't bother him that much. He'd wanted to explain the game to her, but suddenly that didn't seem so important. If she didn't want to listen, he couldn't make her.

He shrugged. "It is. I mean, it may sound silly . . ."

Lizzie laughed. "Are you kidding? Sarah and me used to pretend we were spies for days. Sometimes it's nice to be in a fantasy."

Peter felt his eyebrows furrow. That wasn't what *Elf Mirror* was. It wasn't some kids' game— he had to be a real hero in it.

"It's different from that" was all he said.

Lizzie paused for a minute but then said, "Maybe I can try it sometime?"

Peter looked up at her in surprise. He hadn't thought she liked video games. And looking into her eyes, he realized she didn't. She was just being nice to him.

"Um, yeah. If you want, sometime," he said.

The school came into view, and Peter went silent again. He knew Lizzie was just being Lizzie, but somehow her kindness made him feel worse.

As the four of them approached the school and mingled with the students milling around, Peter felt more alone than ever.

In period 1, during language arts, Peter's world changed.

Right in the middle of a discussion of *The Lion, the Witch, and the Wardrobe*, the most beautiful boy Peter had ever seen walked in.

"Can I help you?" Mr. Moreau asked.

The boy chewed gum and smiled widely. Peter had never seen such white teeth. "Uh, yeah. Kai Delikatua. I'm new."

He was about three inches taller than Peter, and his skin was a rich olive brown—lighter than Peter and Olive's black-brown coloring but darker than Sarah's copper-brown tone, and way darker than Lizzie's pale white. His hair was wavy and dark brown, and Peter could see deep brown eyes under his thick eyebrows. His eyes actually twinkled. When the boy turned his gaze toward him, Peter looked down at his desk quickly.

"All right, Kai. But I'm going to ask you to spit out your gum. No chewing in class." Mr. Moreau smiled and grabbed a small garbage can near his desk. He held it up to Kai.

Kai smiled back, kept chewing, and then blew a bubble. Mr. Moreau stood holding the garbage can, his smile fading until finally his lips formed a straight line.

"Kai . . . ," Mr. Moreau said.

"What? I'm just trying to get as much as I can out of this gum." Kai chewed harder and then smiled at the class. Some of the students snickered. Peter smiled down at his desk, though he felt bad for Mr. Moreau.

"In the garbage can, now, Mr. Delikatua." Mr. Moreau was definitely mad. He only used last names when he lost patience.

Kai chewed one more time and then made a loud gulping sound. He opened his mouth wide and said, "I swallowed it. See? You can quit holding the garbage now, Mr. Morose." Then

he smiled again and pointed to an empty desk catty-corner to and behind Peter. "Should I take that one?"

Mr. Moreau put the garbage can down. "Yes. But you should know that you're already on thin ice—perhaps in your other classes you can begin acting a little more mature. You only have one chance to make a good first impression, Mr. Delikatua, and yours so far leaves a lot to be desired."

Kai turned toward the class and walked to his seat. Peter could see he was chewing gum still. He sat down with a thwump, and Mr. Moreau continued with his discussion of *The Lion, the Witch, and the Wardrobe.*

"So, as we were discussing, the question is: I you think this was a real world the children w

to? Or do you think they made it up together? As a sort of break from the real world? Remember, this was during wartime, when the children felt displaced and as if they didn't belong anywhere."

Kai's voice piped up near Peter. "Oh, it was definitely a real world. I've been there."

Laughs from students twittered around the room.

"Mr. Delikatua . . ."

Kai went on. "I've been to a lot of so-called fantasy worlds. Narnia, Hogwarts, Rivendell. I just got back from the land in *Elf Mirror*, in fact."

Peter sat up straight and turned to look at him. The class laughed while Mr. Moreau frowned, but Peter wanted Kai to talk more

about *Elf Mirror*. He didn't believe Kai had been there, of course; but he knew the game, and maybe he and Peter could talk about it.

Kai saw Peter looking at him and he winked, which made Peter turn around fast, his face hot and flushed.

He realized he'd have to actually be able to look at Kai if he wanted to have a conversation with him. He was just so . . . different from anyone Peter had ever met. No one could or would ignore Kai—he seemed larger than life. He was able to talk to adults like he was on their level. And walk into a room of complete strangers and be okay. Better than okay—he basically owned this room. Even as a new kid, he seemed to fit right in.

Peter couldn't even speak up at a charades

game. With his family, he just went along with everything. Kai didn't seem like the type of person to do that. Not at all. Everyone would listen when Kai talked, Peter was sure of it.

He heard smacking and knew that Kai had started chewing his gum loudly again. Peter laughed a little and smiled to himself—Kai clearly wasn't afraid of anything.

"Mr. Delikatua," Mr. Moreau said. Peter had never heard him so angry. "I asked you to get rid of your gum. As you cannot follow directions, please report to the principal's office."

Peter heard the desk squeak way too loudly. Kai walked by Peter's elbow, and Peter could feel his warmth as he passed. Something about Kai made him sit up straighter.

Kai turned around to face the class, still grin-

ning and chewing gum, and said, "Later, losers."
He caught eyes with Peter and winked again, then
walked out of the room.

Peter very much wanted to get to know him
better.

CHAPTER 3

Peter the Brave

That night, Peter was quieter than usual. Quieter, but with a constant smile on his face.

He played *Elf Mirror* after dinner, thinking of all the things he'd want to talk to Kai about. Peter was only a little way into the game. His avatar had made it through the mirror and he'd met the guide. But she'd asked him for the right spell to get his weapons, and he couldn't figure out how to get all the ingredients. The game was a mix of Peter's favorite things: puzzles to solve, evil creatures to fight, and an awesome world full of magic.

He shut off the game and practiced what he was going to ask Kai: "Have you met the guide? I can't find the fairy weed for the spell." He whispered it over and over until it felt natural on his lips.

Tomorrow he was going to talk to Kai. He could almost see Kai winking at him as he drifted off to sleep.

Going into sixth grade, in a new school, hadn't been easy for Peter. Trying to understand the layout of the school, going to a locker before his classes, and changing teachers constantly had been jarring for him. The halls were loud, and people always bumped into him, like he wasn't even there. Olive seemed to be fine, but it made Peter nervous every day. And it made him dread school just a little bit.

Except today.

He stood at his locker, looking around for Kai. He wanted to catch him before class so he could ask about *Elf Mirror*. He'd practiced all night to start the conversation. It was time to make it happen.

Before first period, Lizzie and Sarah stood by Peter and Olive's locker. Peter could barely pay attention to them.

"Peter!" Olive said loudly, right in his ear.

He snapped back to the conversation the four of them had been having. Well, that the three of them had been having with him standing there.

"What?" he asked, watching more people walk by.

"I was telling you that I took the phone because it's my day and you left it on the table. And then Lizzie asked you a question!" Olive said, her voice irritated and loud.

Lizzie smiled at him. "It's okay. I was just asking if you're coming over with Olive to do some orientation for the orchard tours."

Suddenly, Peter spotted wavy brown hair bobbing above the crowd. His heart started beating wildly.

"Uh, gotta go," he said, and grabbed his books, trying to keep the bobbing hair in his sights. He pushed between people and watched as the hair turned a corner to a different hall-way. He followed.

Behind him, he heard, "Peter, what are you doing?" but he ignored Olive's voice. There was something else in her tone lately, he realized sud-denly. She was hurt. A small pang of guilt made him slow down a little. He almost turned around to say something to her, but when he looked back, he saw Olive, Lizzie, and Sarah talking in a crowded huddle. There was no room for him.

The bell rang, and Peter groaned. He'd missed his chance to talk to Kai before class. Somehow, without even saying a word, Olive and his friends had stopped him from saying what he needed to say—again.

He walked to language arts class, trying to get rid of the frustration he felt. He sat down hard in his seat, already thinking about when he could try to talk to Kai next. Maybe after class? If Kai could make it through without being sent to the principal's office . . . But to Peter's surprise, he didn't need to worry about it. Kai came and slid into the seat near him well before the second bell rang. He hadn't thought a rebel like Kai would get anywhere on time. Peter's mood immediately lifted.

He took a deep breath and steeled his nerve. He would talk to Kai. He would. Surely the looks from the other day meant something, right?

He turned around and caught eyes with Kai. "Where are you in the grame?" he asked.

And then kicked himself. Grame? What was a grame?

"I mean . . . glame," he muttered. "Um. Game.

The *Elf Ear* game. I mean. The *Elf . . .*" His voice trailed off.

Kai grinned. "Ah, Petey, I know what you're talking about."

Peter caught his breath: Kai knew his name! Mostly. Peter had never been called Petey in his life. But it seemed okay coming from Kai.

"I just finally got through the mirror. It was hard, though—took me forever. But the graphics are wicked cool. Now I need to find the spells from the witch and start on the quest to the dragon." Kai leaned forward in his desk, chewing his gum loudly and bouncing his legs, making the desks behind him and in front of him bounce too. The girl in the desk in front of him started giving him a dirty look, but Kai grinned at her and her irritated expression morphed into a dreamy smile.

Peter nodded and turned all the way around in his desk to look at Kai, leaning toward him. "I just got through the mirror too. I'm thinking about going online and getting a partner. I think you might need one to get the spells." He noticed that the people around him were staring at him. He wanted to say, "I know I don't talk a lot. But that doesn't mean I don't have things to say." Instead, he lifted up his chin a little. Somehow talking to Kai made him feel a little bolder.

Kai pointed his finger at Peter like a gun and made a clicking sound as he winked. He blew a bubble. "Well, maybe I'll catch you online and we can partner up."

Peter's stomach flipped. He smiled back and was about to give Kai his username when the second bell rang and Mr. Moreau came in. Without looking up, he said, "Kai, spit your gum out." Kai took his gum out and threw it at the front of the room. It landed directly on Mr. Moreau's desk.

"Sorry, sir," Kai said. "I was totally aiming for the trash can."

Peter noticed that the trash can was in the corner of the room, far away from Mr. Moreau's desk.

The teacher sighed. "Principal's office, Kai."

Kai got up, still grinning, and walked down the row. He rapped his knuckles on Peter's desk and said, "Catch you on the other side," and then breezed out the door.

Peter could swear he felt the air currents still swirling after Kai had left. He put his chin on top of his hands on his desk and tried to cover up the huge smile he couldn't seem to get rid of.

CHAPTER 4

Once Upon a Winter's Night

The Garrisons had been right—the orchard was beautiful in the winter.

Peter stood by the barn, shifting on his feet nervously. The air was frigid, and his breath came out in thick sheets of white. He watched as Tabitha Garrison, Lizzie, Gloria, Olive, and a few of the extra hands the Garrisons hired for the winter season tried to put up lights all around the fences on the property. Except they didn't get very far because every few minutes, someone would get hit with a snowball. As far as Peter could tell, there was no one particular instigator—they were all throwing snowballs at each other.

He watched as Gloria started to yell "ACT—" but was cut off by a snowball in the face. Sarah and Lizzie collapsed in laughter, and Olive and Tabitha high-fived. Peter *sort of* wished he was over there with them, instead of stuck here, having to "face his fears," like his dads said. But at the same time, he liked the feeling of watching from afar and of having the moment to himself. He was secretly glad that Olive had forgotten she'd said she would help with the sleigh rides.

He stamped his feet to keep warm and heard the horses near the barn behind him snort and stamp too. The sound made his stomach do a nervous flip. He heard Albert Garrison talking to someone else in the barn.

"Ah, you're here!" Albert said cheerily—the way he said everything.

Peter recognized the sheriff's voice. "Well, we like to help neighbors in need. We heard you might want to do a practice run with the sleigh and show Peter the ropes. Ms. Shirvani and Luna and me decided we'd sacrifice the evening to help you out. Shoot, Luna—"

A bark sounded near him and Peter jumped. An all-white dog came sprinting out of the barn, headed toward Peter. The dog was hard to see when there was no barn behind her and there was no contrast between her and the snow. Peter thought briefly that he should run, but the dog was there before he could even react.

Peter put his hands up as she jumped on his chest and knocked him down, and he waited for the bite. But instead . . . his face was covered in kisses. Peter found himself giggling a little, even though it was pretty gross and the ground was incredibly cold. And just two seconds before, he'd thought he was going to die.

"Ah, Luna, dang it." Sheriff Hadley appeared over Peter and the dog wriggled off him, her tail going a million miles an hour. Peter shot up and brushed snow off his back. Luna wriggled in a circle all around Sheriff Hadley and Peter—she was clearly too happy to sit still.

Peter could see she was just a puppy. He put his hand out and she came over and leaned into his legs, falling over and landing on top of his feet. Peter giggled. She might be the sweetest dog he'd ever met.

"Peter, I'm so sorry," Sheriff Hadley said as he patted his knee and called Luna to him. "I'm trying to train her, but she's still a little squirrelly. And she likes people. Especially you, by the looks of it."

Footsteps crunched in the snow, and Ms. Shirvani and Albert appeared, smiling. Luna wagged herself over to the newcomers and did circles around them. Ms. Shirvani laughed, and Albert said, "This is one wiggly dog! Her tail seems to be leading her head, instead of the other way around."

"Peter, Albert tells us we have the honor of your sleigh-driving expertise tonight? How fun!" Ms. Shirvani petted Luna, and the horses stamped behind them.

Peter blushed and nodded. Even though his only expertise was in not wanting to be there.

A squeal and a splat sounded from far away, and Peter saw Lizzie sprawled out on the ground, laughing, and Sarah standing over her triumphantly.

"Well, that's my daughter. A warrior. I do hope she takes it easy on Lizzie . . ." Ms. Shirvani's eyes were full of love.

Albert said, "I think Lizzie can hold her own. As can Olive and Peter. You're all pretty well matched, right, Peter?"

Peter nodded, not at all sure if that was true.

"I don't want to rush us, but is that sleigh ready? It's just a tad cold out here," Sheriff Hadley said. Peter was glad. Albert might be one of the nicest parents he'd ever met, but he was definitely spacey. He wouldn't be surprised if Albert forgot why they were all standing around.

"Oh, yes! It's on the other side. During winter break, Peter, I'll show you how to hook it up. But for now, you'll just ride in front with me. Sound good?" Peter nodded again and followed the adults as they walked to the other side of the barn. There a beautiful, ornate sleigh stood, attached to one horse. The horse snorted, and white air came from his nose.

Peter had a thought. "Does the . . . is the horse

okay with pulling this?" Then he blushed again. Maybe it was a dumb question and he should have kept quiet. But he'd hate to think of any animal being forced into doing something they didn't want to do.

Albert patted his shoulder. "That's always a good question. This is Sebastian, and Sebastian loves to run and to work. He gets really antsy if we can't ride him and let him run. So this he likes— he pulls the sleigh and it helps him get some of that energy out." He winked at Peter. "But you should always ask a horse if they want to work. And listen to their answer."

Peter's eyebrows furrowed. "But how do you . . . ?"

"Okay, dear riders, shall we go?" Albert said loudly. "Your sleigh awaits!"

Luna and Sebastian were sniffing each other, and Sebastian did a few side steps. If Peter asked him what he felt right now, he was pretty sure Sebastian would say, "That dog is way too rambunctious."

And sure enough, Sebastian kept trying to pull the sleigh away from Luna. He moved a couple of steps forward and the sleigh slid on its runners.

"I'm so excited about this!" Ms. Shirvani said. Then she and Sheriff Hadley exchanged a look that Peter could only describe as mushy.

They climbed into the sleigh. It was partially covered because of the cold, so that the guests sat under a sort of hood. But the drivers in front were exposed, and Peter tightened his scarf and hid his face in it. He could feel the energy of Sebastian traveling through the sleigh—he seemed so powerful. Peter's stomach flipped again.

He hoped Sebastian was a *nice* powerful.

Albert seemed to notice Peter's nervousness. He said quietly, "Sebastian has been working with us for a long time. We talked about giving you a nice smooth ride today." Then he picked up the reins. "The reins tell Sebastian when to go and how fast. We only use them to guide him and give him a little nudge to go faster, or a little pull to slow down. Got it? Though by this point, it's pretty much like Sebastian understands English."

Peter nodded and swallowed.

"Ready?" Albert asked the sheriff and Ms. Shirvani.

Luna barked once like she was answering. Both the sheriff and Ms. Shirvani replied "Yes," laughing.

Peter still had some doubts about the horse liking what he was doing. Surely pulling along what looked like a heavy sleigh with three adults, a kid, and a dog was too hard. And it felt kind of mean.

But all Albert said was "Let's go, Sebastian. Let's see the forest!" and the sleigh was off. Right away, Albert had to pull on the reins to get Sebastian to slow down. Peter relaxed a little. The horse really did seem to be enjoying it.

And Peter had to admit, as he looked around, that he was enjoying it too.

The sun was still up but was just starting to

fade a tiny bit. That made all the snow look sparkly and magical. The Garrisons' orchard butted up against a huge, beautiful forest, and the sleigh slid by the edge of it, so that Peter could look in. Sunlight filtered through the trees, and snowflakes danced in the beams.

It had started to snow.

No one talked as the sleigh raced across the snow. The sound lulled Peter into an almost dozey state. They turned down a large and well-worn path through the forest—Sebastian didn't even have to be told where to go. He'd clearly gone down the path a million times.

The snow floated down, and the sun began to set just a little more. Peter felt like he was in a trance or a fairy tale. The world seemed so magical and full of possibility . . . but at the same time serene and blissful. He wanted to do this every day.

But the reverie was broken by a bark from Luna. Peter felt the sleigh shift and then saw a white streak take off into the forest.

Sheriff Hadley yelled, "LUNA!" and Albert pulled on the reins to get Sebastian to stop. The horse stopped, but the sleigh moved forward on the snow. Finally, the whole thing stopped moving and the sheriff jumped out.

He called, "LUNA!" again near the edge of the trees, his hand cupped at the side of his mouth. Peter felt the sleigh shift again as Ms. Shirvani got out.

"Colin, we should look for the tracks," Peter heard her say. The sheriff nodded, his eyebrows furrowed with worry.

And then they heard a yelp, like Luna was hurt. Was being hurt.

After that, everything moved so fast that later, Peter wouldn't remember exactly how it all happened. He saw the sheriff tear off into the woods and immediately fall down; saw Ms. Shirvani follow him; heard another terrifying yelp from the woods; and watched as Albert got out of the sleigh to go help the sheriff and Ms. Shirvani.

"Stay here, Peter, I'll be right back," Albert said as he stepped down from the sleigh and hurried toward the trees.

Leaving the reins on the seat by Peter.

As Peter picked them up, another yelp from Luna sounded close to the sleigh. So close it scared Peter.

So close it also scared Sebastian.

The horse reared up, making the reins slide off the seat. And then he took off down the path at full speed, a terrified Peter hanging on for dear life.

CHAPTER 5

The Woods Are Lovely, Dark, and

Peter heard shouts behind h
grew farther and farther awa
helplessly as Sebastian tore c
The snow had started coming ha
Peter had a giddy moment of think
tiful everything was. If he hadn't b
out of control, he would have lov
shushing sound of the sleigh's
through the snow, the huffs of Seb

Suddenly, a rabbit appeared in the middle of the path. Sebastian swerved, now taking the sleigh and Peter through the trees. Branches whipped past Peter's head and he ducked this way and that. He called out to Sebastian, but his voice was carried away by the wind and it was almost like he'd said nothing at all. Trees shushed by him in blurs.

Except for one tree.

The branch came out of nowhere and caught Peter right on the temple. Sebastian was going so fast that even though the contact was minimal, the speed of the sleigh made the touch a slam, and Peter tumbled off the seat. One second he was watching, terrified, as Sebastian and the sleigh tore through the trees. And the next he felt a blinding pain and saw the ground rushing up to meet him.

He lay in the snow for a minute, listening to

the horse and sleigh crashing through the trees, the sound moving farther and farther away. He tried to catch his breath. His head throbbed, and when he put his gloved hand up to touch it, the glove slipped and Peter knew it was blood. Sure enough, when he looked at his glove, it was streaked in red.

He wondered how hard that branch had hit him, to make his head bleed even through a winter hat.

He sat up, but the world spun dangerously, so he lay back down again. Off in the distance he thought he heard a crash, but he couldn't be sure. He took stock of his situation.

He didn't know where he was. He didn't know how far Sebastian had taken him.

He was alone in the woods at night. . . .

And then Peter groaned out loud. A tendril of panic wrapped around him.

It was snowing. So the tracks Sebastian had left would be covered.

Peter tried not to cry. He tried to think about what Olive would do in this situation. Or what his dads would do. Or Tabitha. But all he could feel was the throbbing in his head. And now the cold of the snow seeping through his winter gear.

First things first: find somewhere warm.

He sat up again, this time much more slowly. When he was upright, he blinked a few times until the world righted itself. The woods came into focus, the bright snow underneath him and the dark trees in front of him. Luckily, the sky had the pink tinge it often had when it snowed, so the forest wasn't so dark that he couldn't see. Still, he was desperately aware of every rustle and crack he heard around him.

He thought for a minute. Would it be faster to

try to follow Sebastian or to try to get back to the path?

Peter got slowly to his feet, hanging on to a nearby tree. He felt like he was going to throw up at any moment. The dizziness overtook him for a second, and his vision went black. Then it cleared and he looked around.

Everything looked the same.

The snow around him was pristine—no way to see where Sebastian's and the sleigh's tracks led deeper into the forest. And nothing that could give him his bearings toward the path, either.

Now Peter did cry.

He hadn't ever felt this alone. This alone or in danger. He desperately wished he could hear Olive tell him what to do, or hear Sarah come up with some harebrained scheme, or listen to Lizzie telling him everything would be okay. He wished his dads were there.

He sniffled. Crying was hurting his head, and the cold made his nose hurt. He had to move. Maybe he could find some sort of shelter to hide out in until the morning. Already his fingers felt stiff, and the blood on his hat was freezing.

He started walking. And for the first time ever, he started talking to himself out loud. Somehow it made him feel better.

"Okay, Peter. Just keep going straight. Look for a fallen log or something. Or maybe even Sebastian and the sleigh, because he'd have to stop running sometime, right? Don't think about how cold your feet are. Or your hands. Or how much your head hurts . . ."

He said these things to himself for what felt like hours, until he was too tired to move anymore. He stopped and looked around. To his left, he saw a fallen tree, and though there wasn't a whole lot of shelter there, he thought it would be a good place to rest for just a minute.

He just had to rest.

Peter climbed into the crook formed by the trunk of the fallen tree and one of its huge branches. He scooted down until the wind was mostly blocked. He pulled his legs up into his chest and felt his eyes get heavy.

Somewhere in the back of his head, he heard a warning that he shouldn't fall asleep. But he was too tired. He just needed to close his eyes for a minute. He watched the snow float down—it had let up now and had that magical quality he loved so much. It twirled in spirals, dancing around itself in beautiful patterns. An owl hooted somewhere.

Peter closed his eyes.

CHAPTER 6
It's Just a Game . . . Right?

Peter's eyes snapped open. He thought he'd heard someone call his name. He scrambled to his feet and looked around. His head didn't hurt at all, and he felt no dizziness. The sky still had the tinge of pink, but it seemed to sparkle now. The air was cold, but not frigid anymore.

He scanned the trees, squinting. Far away, he thought he saw . . . smoke. Smoke from a chimney. Could it be?

He walked toward the smoke, making sure to look all around him. It was strange; he didn't feel scared anymore, not even a little bit. In fact, this felt like a great adventure all of a sudden. He thought, vaguely, about his dads worrying. But then he thought that if that smoke really did belong to a house, he'd be able to call them soon. Just his luck that it was Olive's day for their cell phone.

He had barely walked for any length of time when the trees thinned and he stepped into a clearing. Sure enough, a small cottage with warm, glowing lights sat in the middle of it, smoke wafting from the small chimney. Peter could smell something delicious—some sort of stew, maybe—and his mouth watered. He hadn't realized how hungry he was. Thirsty, too.

He walked up to the cottage and knocked. He briefly thought that was unlike him— normally he'd try to suss out the situation before he made any moves. But he didn't feel any danger about anything at the moment. The cottage, the clearing, the smells . . . all of it was just right somehow.

No one answered on the first knock. There had to be someone there.

He knocked again. Nothing.

Peter walked around the cottage and tried to look in the windows, but they were all steamy and hard to see through. He couldn't see anyone.

He went back to the front door and thought for a moment. This wasn't his house. He was a visitor. It was rude to just walk in. But . . . it was cold outside. And he was so hungry and thirsty.

Plus, everything seemed so magical right now—it had to be safe.

He pressed down on the door handle and the door swung inward. He stood there for a second, taking in the space.

The cottage had a small sitting room to the left where a cozy sofa sat, piled with blankets, in front of a crackling fire. The light danced on the walls and on the ceiling. There were books piled around the worn couch, and knitting in a basket sat beside one of the ornate legs.

To his right was a small table in a small kitchen. An old-fashioned stove—the kind he and Olive had seen on a "living history" field trip—glowed, and on it stood a black iron pot that had steam coming out of it. Definitely stew. Cups and bowls and plates sat on the open shelves, and everywhere there were plants. Dried, living, sitting all around . . . the whole place seemed like a bit of a greenhouse.

"Well, don't let all the heat out! It's about time you got here. We have to get going," said a voice to the left. A voice that Peter recognized.

He turned to the couch again and there, having appeared out of nowhere, sat Kai.

Peter stammered, "Uh . . . wh-what?"

Kai stood up impatiently and grabbed Peter's arm. "Come in! You're making me cold. And we need to get going."

He ushered Peter in and shut the door behind him. "Plus, I'm guessing you'll want to eat first."

Peter blinked and tried to collect his thoughts. The boy in front of him was definitely Kai—same smile, same voice, same everything. He wore all white and had a white scarf wrapped around his neck. But he seemed to sparkle, too, just like the sky. Not sparkle, exactly. Just . . . glow.

Peter flashed back to a Community Spirit at the town hall where they talked about the different afterlives different religions believed in. He thought he remembered hearing something about all white . . . an angelic presence . . .

Peter swallowed. Was he dead? And was this his afterlife?

Kai had started dishing up stew into two bowls. He set them down on the table and began eating his with gusto.

"Am . . . I, uh . . . Am I dead?" Peter asked, his voice shaking a little.

Kai put his spoon down and laughed. "No,

you big dork! Not yet, anyway. We have to go on the quest. It took you long enough to get here. I've waited forever."

Peter sank down into a chair at the table, relieved. The smell of the stew wafted up to him and his stomach growled. He took off his coat, hat, and gloves, picked up the spoon, and took a big bite of the stew. It was the most delicious meal he had ever tasted. And he was used to eating food Albert Garrison cooked, which was saying something. Soon he felt warm all over and very full.

And full of questions.

Kai had sat back in his chair and was looking at Peter with amusement. Peter wondered if this was the only expression he could make. But it didn't matter—it looked good on him.

Peter started, "Okay, what quest? Where am I? Can I use your phone? Do you live out here? Why have you been waiting for me? Does someone else live—"

Kai put up his hand, laughing. "You're so funny, Peter. But we don't have time for this. Come on, let's get to the mirror." With that, he stood up and beckoned Peter to follow him.

"I really need to use your phone," Peter said, following.

Kai snorted. "Does it look like there's a phone in here?"

Peter looked around. It did not, in fact, look like there was a phone in there.

"Do you have your cell phone? It's Olive's day—"

Kai stopped abruptly. Peter realized they'd walked down a hall that seemed much longer than the cottage seemed big. That was strange.

But what about this wasn't?

They were in some sort of room—another room, like a library. More books sat on the floor and on bookshelves, and candles lit up the gloom. There were no windows in the room. Just a tall piece of furniture with a cloth draped over it that they stopped in front of.

"Here it is. We gotta go. The dragon is ruthless." Kai pulled the cloth from the piece of furniture, and Peter gasped.

A mirror. A mirror that looked like a real-life version of the Elf Mirror from his video game.

"Are we . . . inside the video game?" Peter asked, completely confused.

Kai laughed hard. "No, silly. This is real. Where do you think they got the idea for the video game?"

He looked intensely at Peter. "I was right about you, right? You're the right person to go on this quest with me?"

Peter hesitated, then nodded. He didn't know what being the "right person" meant, to be honest. He just knew he wanted to see where this mirror took them. And to get closer to Kai.

Kai slapped his shoulder and grinned. "I knew it! I knew there was something special about you. I saw it the first time I laid eyes on you."

He turned to the mirror and said, "All right then, no time to waste."

Then he took a giant step and went through the mirror, leaving Peter standing there staring at his own confused expression.

CHAPTER 7
The Quest

Peter blinked a few times at the mirror. Like water, it had made a wave when Kai went through, and then it stopped, turning back into a regular old mirror.

Peter blinked again.

He thought about all the times he'd read about kids who had encountered another world, or a gateway to another world. How he'd push them along in his head: "Come on! Just go through already!"

But now he understood.

This was not the normal state of things. He had no idea what would happen if he put his leg in. What if he got stuck? What if he went to a different world that was awful?

He shook off his hesitation. Kai had gone through the mirror. So could he.

He put his finger out and touched the mirror. It was cold, so cold he wished he had his gloves on still. The mirror rippled. He just needed to step through, exactly like Kai had.

Peter took a deep breath. And then stepped through the mirror.

The sensation was like jumping into a freezing pool on a hot day. But it didn't last long, because soon Peter felt the sun on his back and could smell honeysuckle on the breeze. And something else that he didn't recognize but liked very much. He had landed belly-down, and he felt the earth with his hands. Spring. It was spring here.

"Hey!" Peter heard as he got up and wiped his hands on his pants.

His pants seemed weird. When he looked down, he saw that they were made of leather and hides, like he'd hunted some poor animal. He didn't like that.

"What took you so long?" Kai came up beside him. Peter caught a glimpse of a tall girl with long dark hair and pointed ears walking away.

Pointed ears!

An elf. Kai had been talking to an elf.

"Um . . . ," Peter said. Kai looked at him expectantly. "What is this place? It really looks like the land in *Elf Mirror*."

Kai's eyebrows furrowed. "What are you talking about? This is Tiar. And they need help. You're going to help me get rid of the dragon. He's fierce and ruthless and we need strong people to defeat him. I've been waiting for you to show up so we could get going." Kai's frown deepened. "I thought you said you were the right person to come with me on this quest."

Before Peter could say anything, a terrible roar sounded, like the loudest airplane he'd ever heard. It made the ground shake. He saw in the distant mountains a column of smoke and fire shooting straight up into the sky.

Kai scowled. He seemed nothing like the smart-aleck kid Peter had seen in class. "He's getting restless," Kai said. "We either need to give him a tribute of fifty people, or he will ransack towns and villages and eat everyone. Unless we can defeat him."

Peter shook his head. "Wait. I don't understand. I have a lot of questions."

The girl with dark hair came back, this time riding a horse and pulling along two others. She looked almost identical to Sarah. Only a Sarah with pointed ears. Peter stared.

"Well, here are the horses. We'd better get going now to see the witch. We want to make it there before sundown."

Peter took a step back. "Sarah?"

The girl blinked. "What's a 'sarah'?" She looked at Kai.

Kai grinned, finally looking like the boy Peter knew from class. "Peter, this is Lithliel. She's a warrior here in Tiar. She and other warriors have tried to defeat the dragon, but failed."

Sarah-not-Sarah said, "Thanks for the reminder." She dropped the horses' reins and then said, "Okay, get on your horses. We've chatted enough. Let's go." Kai moved to get on his horse. But Peter couldn't take it anymore. He had to speak up.

"WAIT!" he yelled.

Lithliel and Kai stopped moving and stared at him in surprise.

Peter went on, "I need to know what's going on! I need answers. Where are we? Why are we here? Why were you waiting for me? Why is a dragon trying to hurt everyone? Why do you think we can do anything about it if Lithliel and other warriors can't? Why do we have to ride horses?" The last question made Peter cringe a little. He hadn't meant to let them know how scared he was of riding the horse.

Kai and Lithliel stared at him.

"I mean, if you don't mind . . ." Peter's voice trailed off.

"This is who you brought?" Lithliel said to Kai.

But Kai only said, "Come on, let's go. We'll go to the witch and she'll explain everything."

Peter felt himself burning with shame. He wasn't quite sure why Kai had brought him either. And when he thought about getting on the horse, his self-doubt grew dragon-sized.

But Kai and Lithliel were waiting. And they had a witch to go to, evidently. He hoped she was a nice witch. He hoped this was a nice horse.

He had a lot of hopes.

Peter walked up to the horse, trying to take

big deep breaths like his dads had taught him. The horse was beautiful and black, with a mane and tail that were almost rainbow-hued. Peter looked the horse in the eye and petted him gently. The horse moved and Peter tensed, but he stood his ground. Then he realized that the horse was moving toward him, not away. He must not hate it that Peter was petting him. Peter relaxed just a little and whispered, "Will you be nice to me?"

The horse snorted like he was saying yes. Peter smiled at the thought and felt his body relax even more. "What's your name?" he whispered.

He didn't know how he knew, but he just did: the horse's name was Samson. Peter felt giddy and almost light-headed again. He petted Samson some more.

"Albert says I should ask horses if they want to work. So . . . do you want to go on a quest with me? I don't know what it's about yet. But I guess I will soon. Can I ride you?" Samson snorted, and Peter knew that was a definite yes. He smiled, and for the first time since entering this world, he felt a little confident.

He put his foot in the stirrup, took a deep breath, and swung his leg over Samson. The horse moved a little while he was swinging, but Peter landed with a thump on the saddle. Samson snorted. Peter was pretty sure it was an approving snort.

Peter could feel Samson practically vibrating underneath him. He took a deep breath and smelled the horsey smell, felt Samson shift his weight, and looked around from his new height.

Things looked pretty cool from up here. Peter patted Samson on the neck and looked at Lithliel and Kai. "I'm ready. Let's go find this witch," he said, holding on to the reins the way his horseback-riding instructor from long ago had taught him.

Kai grinned and said, "Finally." He and Lithliel nudged their horses and they set off. Samson followed. At first, a zing of fear pinged through Peter when they started moving, but then he found the rhythm—the backward-and-forward movement, the feeling of the wind in his hair, the sound of hooves on dirt. There was nothing like this. He felt like he and Samson had been riding together forever.

They passed along a path in the forest, a lot like the path he and Sebastian had traveled down. Or had run down, really. But here the flowers were in bloom and the trees waved to them. There was a smell of earth after a rain, deeper in the forest, and of horses and flowers. Peter was reminded of the first time he saw the orchard—it all felt so magical to him.

Samson followed Lithliel and Kai without Peter's even having to nudge him. Pretty soon the elation of riding a horse faded away a bit, and Peter remembered:

They were going to see a witch.

He really hoped she was nice.

CHAPTER 8
Something Familiar

Peter, Lithliel, and Kai rode for what felt like forever along the endless forest path. The trees loomed large and seemed ancient, and as much as Peter loved the forest, he was happy to come to a clearing.

He saw the cottage first, a few yards away, almost like it had just appeared. It looked a little like the Garrisons' house, only a lot smaller and more cottage-y. It was surrounded by bushes and herbs and flowers of all sorts—Peter could smell something delicate and sweet. But the thing he most noticed was the shimmering. The whole cottage shimmered.

A tendril of smoke wafted out of the chimney. As Peter looked on, the smoke turned from white, to red, to pink, to blue. Suddenly, a pang of fear shot through him.

"Does she . . . ," Peter started, but then lost his voice. He tried again. "Does she know we're coming?"

Lithliel looked impatient. "Of course she does. She's the witch." She climbed down from her horse and said, "We can walk from here. It's nice the witch is so close. Last time, I had to go to the bottom of the river."

Peter did a double take. "What? What do you mean?"

Lithliel snorted. "Well, she doesn't stay in one place, does she? She has to move around, otherwise she'd get no peace."

Peter decided not to push it. Still, he couldn't help but ask, "But under a river?"

Kai started walking. "Well, she's straight ahead now. Let's go."

They reached the cottage door, and Peter waited until Samson came to a complete stop and then climbed down. He still felt awkward about riding, but he didn't feel scared at all. He took a minute to smile to himself—horses were actually kind of cool.

He tied the reins to a small wooden fence

around the huge garden, patted Samson on the neck, and watched as Kai and Lithliel tied up their horses as well. The three of them looked at each other. Without saying a word, they walked down the path to the door of the cottage.

The smell of herbs was strong—Peter could smell mint and basil, some sort of flower, and an earthy scent that smelled heavenly. He instantly loved this place.

The door opened before anyone knocked. Peter said, "Hello?"

"Come in, come in!" said a voice that sounded a lot like Lizzie's. Peter, Kai, and Lithliel walked in, and Peter got a good look at the girl in the purple robe.

Actually, she wasn't a girl—she was a woman.

But she looked young and had a sparkle in her eyes. She had pale skin and red hair, and she smiled hugely when she saw everyone.

"I'm glad your trip has been uneventful. I hope so, because from here on out, you will only have events." She laughed and put a kettle on the stove. Peter saw that it was a stove exactly like the one in the cottage he had met Kai in. That felt like ages ago—lifetimes, even.

"Can I get you some tea?" the woman asked.

Peter nodded, and Kai and Lithliel said, "Yes, please."

It occurred to Peter that he was standing in a witch's house. Fairy tales and movies came rushing into his head. Were they in trouble? Here he was in a new world with new people. And he voluntarily had gone to a witch's house. It occurred to him that that might not have been the brightest of ideas.

He swallowed and cleared his throat. "Excuse me, but are you . . . a . . . uh . . . good witch?" he asked. His voice sounded more uncertain than he wanted it to be.

The witch let out a loud, long, mirthful laugh. Lithliel shook her head, and Kai looked embarrassed. Peter once again felt shame. But he needed to ask—what if they were all in danger?

"Oh, dear. I see the propaganda has gotten to you. It's not your fault, you darling boy." The kettle began to boil and whistle. "You can call me Mariel, if that's more comfortable than thinking of me as 'the witch.'"

Kai whispered, "Peter, why would you ask that?"

Mariel answered, "Oh, Kai, don't blame him. People have always been afraid of witches. They don't understand, so they make up horrible stories. That's in the other world, though. The world Peter is from. It takes a true soul to look past the noise of other voices and flashy things. It takes a keen heart to understand who a person really is. To listen to what a person is at their core." She poured water into four cups and added sachets. Immediately, the cottage smelled even more strongly of mint and basil, and a hint of cherry. She handed a cup to Peter. "Take a moment, dear. Close your eyes. Listen to your heart. What is it saying about me?"

Peter closed his eyes. But he felt self-conscious and opened them again. "But what am I listening for?"

Mariel said, "You'll know it. Take a deep breath. Be still. Listen to yourself."

Peter swallowed. He took a deep breath, closed his eyes, and let his mind go blank. After a few seconds, the thought of Mariel came into his mind. He felt warm all over; taken care of. He felt goodness. He smiled.

Then Lithliel came into his mind. He felt kindness, but ferocity, too. A heart of justice and righteous fighting.

Kai popped into his head. And he felt . . . nothing.

His eyes flew open. Mariel stared at him with knowing eyes. "Ah, excellent. I think you've heard what you need to hear, dear. Now come sit down at this table, you three. We have a strategy to discuss."

Peter's unease had come back, but now it was because he wasn't sure what had just happened. Kai had been nothing but fantastic to him. Maybe there was something wrong with Peter that he couldn't listen to his heart, as Mariel had said, and feel Kai's essence.

Mariel began talking. "Peter will want to know what is happening, I imagine. So first, I will talk about Tiar. Does that sound good, Peter?"

Peter nodded. Kai sighed, and Peter heard the impatience in it. Lithliel began picking up knickknacks and examining them like they were treasures, but Mariel didn't seem to mind.

"Tiar is a land of magic and elves, Peter, much different from your world. And unlike your world, there are many, many warriors. Like our Lithliel here." Lithliel dropped a ceramic cat at the mention of her name but immediately caught it. She nodded, and Peter had to stop himself from smiling.

"But I'm the best warrior," Lithliel said.

"That you are, dear," Mariel said.

Kai said, elbowing Lithliel, "Only not good enough to kill the dragon." He winked at her.

Lithliel smiled a little, but Peter could see that Kai's remark had hurt her feelings. Kai seemed to be oblivious. Maybe Peter could mention it to him when they had a minute alone . . .

Mariel watched Peter and took a sip of tea. "It's true. This dragon is more intractable than any we've had before. Even my magic and my words are useless against her. And she is demanding fifty elven tributes or else she says she'll destroy us all. Which is why the Witch's Council put out a call to another world for heroes. It seems this problem needs a different solution from what we can provide."

Peter furrowed his eyebrows. "A call? Like, an ad somewhere? And what do you mean, heroes?"

Kai sat up straighter. "That's where I come in. I heard the call and I waited for you in the cottage. You can help me slay this dragon." He leaned over and whispered into Peter's ear, "I've heard there's a huge reward if we do it."

It made sense—it seemed like Kai was familiar with this world. Like he was already a warrior here. He just needed a sidekick. Peter was used to being a sidekick—it was always Olive who saved the day. It was always Olive who spoke for them both and took charge. Peter could be a sidekick to Kai. No problem. He didn't really care about a reward. But he could be helpful. Still, a part of him somewhere deep inside felt . . . disappointed. He wished Mariel hadn't taught him to listen to himself. It just made problems.

Mariel was quiet for a moment, looking into her tea and sloshing it around in the cup. She had a strange look on her face, but then she said, "Yes, the call brought you both here. And there is a reward should you save the town. But first, you'll need some background. You see, the dragon hasn't always been a dragon." She took a sip of her tea. "There are many reasons she grew into what she is and is threatening all. Your task is to find out why. When you find out why, you'll find her true name. If you speak it to her, she will return to who she was. This is one way to solve this problem."

Kai and Lithliel exchanged looks. "Or . . . we could just, uh, destroy her," Lithliel said.

Mariel trained her eyes on Lithliel. "You could."

Kai shifted in his seat. "I mean, she's threatening people. She deserves to be slain. It's that simple."

But something in Peter twinged. Mariel had made it clear that there was more than met the eye with this dragon. He wasn't so sure it was black and white. He felt like he should say something, but he couldn't get out any words.

Everyone was quiet for a second. Then Kai said, somewhat impatiently, "Do you have a magic spell that will help put her to sleep? And allow us to kill her before she eats everyone? That's why I'm here."

Mariel got up and took her teacup to the

small sink. "How you save people is up to you." She bent down near the stove and pulled out a box. She opened it and took out a small bag filled with something. "I will give you this sleeping powder," she said. "If you can get close enough to her to make the powder airborne, it will put her to sleep, and only her. And when she's asleep, you can pierce her heart with a spear or arrow. But," and she looked at Peter as she said this, "you may find you'll want to take a different approach. Follow your heart. Listen to yourself. You'll know what to do."

Lithliel stood up. "Okay," she said, a little too loudly. "We know what to do." As if on cue, a loud roar rattled the windows in the cottage and shook the ground. "We should probably get going."

Mariel gave Peter a big hug and said, "Good

luck. I trust you'll do the right thing."

And with that, the cottage and everything around them disappeared, leaving them standing by their now-free horses and blinking in the sunlight.

CHAPTER 9
The Village

Another roar shook the ground. Far off in the mountains, a column of fire shot through the air.

That didn't seem good.

Lithliel, Kai, and Peter all looked at each other. Peter said, "The dragon." He walked to Samson, patted his neck, and climbed on. Kai and Lithliel climbed onto their horses too.

Peter asked, "How long until we reach the mountain?"

Lithliel shrugged. "Not long. We have to go through a village and then it's a straight ride to there."

Peter swallowed. He'd thought this would take a few days. Maybe even weeks. Every book he'd ever read told him the journey would be the long part. He wasn't sure he was ready to see a dragon quite yet.

Kai's expression was grim. "We'd better get going. We have the sleeping powder, we have a plan . . . No use waiting around. Hiyah!" He kicked his horse and took off. Lithliel grinned at Peter, and he could see her excitement glowing. As a warrior, she was probably really excited about this part. Peter, however, felt a little less than thrilled.

But Samson shifted on his feet, clearly eager to go. So Peter nudged him, and they took off after Kai and Lithliel.

Cantering with a horse was much different from walking, and Peter's fear returned. He pulled on the reins a little and Samson slowed down to a trot. But the trotting felt uncomfortable and Kai and Lithliel started to get smaller and smaller, so Peter took a deep breath, squeezed his legs together, and nudged the horse. Samson responded immediately. After a few minutes, Peter felt the rhythm of the canter and could match his body to Samson's movement. He was amazed at how much could be communicated without saying a word. And at how much he remembered from horseback-riding camp. Samson was all power, and here he was listening to Peter. For the

first time in a long while, Peter felt really heard—
and he hadn't said a thing.

In a short time, Peter saw the village ahead.
Kai and Lithliel had stopped on a hill, and Peter
and Samson soon joined them. The three stood
and looked at the cottages below.

The village looked a little like Main Street in
New Amity, only with thatched-roof cottages. It
immediately made Peter feel at home. Without
speaking, Kai nudged his horse forward, and
they walked down the hill, Lithliel following, then
Peter. As they drew near the first cottage, all three
of them slid off their horses and began walking.

A person with a wheelbarrow waved as they
came closer to the cottage. Peter saw that this was
an elf, but an elf a little different from Lithliel.
This elf was short and jolly-looking, wearing a

green vest. Lithliel was tall and fierce-looking. As Peter looked down the road and glimpsed other elves, he saw that they were all fairly similar. They seemed to be a cross between Keebler elves and elves from *The Lord of the Rings*.

"Are these elves different from you?" he asked Lithliel.

She frowned. "What do you mean?"

"I don't know. They look different?" Peter said.

She shrugged. "Do all humans look alike?"

Peter smiled. "No, we don't."

"So there you have it," she said.

They reached the first cottage, and the elf with the wheelbarrow approached them. He looked a lot like Hakeem from New Amity. His wide smile and welcoming wave reminded Peter of Hakeem too.

"You're here!" said the elf as they walked up to him. "You must be the warriors we've heard so much about."

Peter blushed. The thought of anyone talking about him made him feel exposed. But also a little proud, maybe? Mostly like he hoped he wouldn't let them down.

"I know you're going on a long journey. Can I get you a pastry for the ride?" the elf asked. "Oh, and I'm Habrium."

Lithliel grinned. "I've heard of you, Habrium the baker. And yes, I think we would all love a pastry."

Habrium disappeared into his cottage and reappeared almost immediately, carrying three steaming, leaf-wrapped packages. He handed one to each of them.

He smiled at Peter as he took the pastry. "We all wish you luck. Mariel has said such good things about you. You're Peter, right?"

Peter blushed again, but nodded. Habrium patted him on the shoulder. "This is a lot to take on. Be careful, okay?"

Peter nodded again, and because he wasn't sure what to say, he took a bite of the pastry.

It was like nothing he'd ever tasted before. The bite seemed to spread happiness through his whole body. He looked over at Kai and Lithliel and could see they felt the same way as they took their first bites.

"This is amazing," he said, unable to stop himself. He said it around the huge bite instead of waiting to swallow, and if Olive had been there, she would have smacked him on the shoulder.

Suddenly, and from out of nowhere, Peter felt sad. He missed his sister and best friend. It seemed strange to be on this quest alone. Even if it meant that for once, he was able to make his own decisions. And to speak for himself.

"Thank you," Lithliel said, and Peter echoed her. Kai said, "We have to get going," and started walking.

Habrium grabbed Peter's hand. "Good luck, Peter. All our hopes are with you. But please know—this dragon is the toughest to ever menace our land. Be careful. Take care of yourselves."

Peter nodded. He tried to swallow his fear. The toughest dragon ever? That didn't sound good. He hoped the other dragons were as tough as kittens.

They continued through the village, the

smells of cooking food and burning iron reaching him. He saw a blacksmith's forge ahead of them, near the market and toward the end of the road. As they walked, townspeople waved to them and cheered. The elves looked suspiciously like the people in New Amity: there was a Stella look-alike; an Annabelle; a Rachel and a Dinah and an Aaron, plus a tiny elf baby, as well as a Dani look-alike . . . He even saw a couple of elves who looked like Tabitha and Albert Garrison and a really dramatic-seeming elf who looked like Gloria.

"Am I in *The Wizard of Oz*?" he muttered to himself. The old movie was a favorite in his household. He suddenly felt like Dorothy.

"What's that?" Kai asked, his eyebrows furrowing. "You should speak up. Did you say

Wizard of Oz? Are there wizards here too, Lithliel?"

Lithliel shook her head. "We haven't had a wizard here in over two centuries. Which isn't horrible. I've heard they get irritated easily."

Peter shook his head. "No, sorry. I'm talking about a movie. A girl gets lost in a tornado and then she's in a different land and everyone looks like someone she knows . . ." But Peter trailed off. Kai's face was scrunched in confusion. And Lithliel said, "What's a movie?"

"Uh, never mind," Peter said, and kept walking, watching the elves around him wave to them. He waved back every once in a while, but self-consciously.

Kai's voice behind him said, "There was no tornado. Are you feeling okay?"

"I'm fine. Just need to find my heart, brain, and courage, I guess," Peter said, and then smiled as Lithliel and Kai frowned at him. For some reason, he found it pretty funny that they had no idea what he was talking about.

They came upon what seemed to be an open market, and the food smell was overwhelming. Peter's mouth watered, even though he'd just had the delicious pastry. Bread and some type of meat and maybe some cheese smell filled the air. He wished he was hungry still—he would have loved to try every food there.

But the three of them walked their horses quickly through the market. Here and there an elf would stop them and shake their hands. Cries of "Thank goodness for you!" and "Be careful!"

rang out. Peter had never felt more visible. It made him uncomfortable, but it also strengthened his resolve: he had to help these elves. Especially since they all seemed so similar to the people in New Amity. In the short time he'd lived there, the people in the town had become important to him. He loved his community, and he would do anything to help them out. He would do the same for these elves.

Finally they came to the edge of the market, and they got onto their horses. The mountain stood in the distance, but somehow way too close. As if on cue, as if the dragon could see them, they heard a huge roar that made the ground shake. Peter looked back at the elves in the market. They were all ducking, some of them hiding under their tables. He hated to see them so scared. And though he, too, was scared, Peter knew it was time to help.

Kai, Lithliel, and Peter looked at each other.

Peter, tamping down his fear, said, "Let's go." He nudged Samson and they took the lead.

CHAPTER 10

The Dragon

As they rode to the mountain—which seemed to be getting closer way too fast—the words Mariel had said kept echoing in Peter's ears: "You'll know what to do."

Peter wasn't so sure. He rarely knew what to do. Didn't Olive always speak for him? Didn't everyone talk over him? Didn't his dads think he couldn't do anything?

He looked at Kai, who was now in front of him.

Lithliel was in front of Kai, leading the group to the place where the dragon lived. If Peter could just be more like Kai . . . Kai didn't seem to be unsure of anything. He seemed to know exactly what to say and what to do. He hadn't hesitated once during this whole adventure.

And Kai was counting on Peter to be a good sidekick. Somewhere, deep inside Peter, something squirmed at the word "sidekick." Still, he would be lucky enough to do that right.

As if he sensed Peter looking, Kai turned around and said, "I don't know what the witch was talking about. But I think she isn't thinking right. We have to kill the dragon. She's going to eat everyone—it's the sensible thing to do."

Peter swallowed but didn't say anything. He leaned over and petted Samson to buy some time.

Somehow, he couldn't disagree with Kai. He didn't want to lose Kai as a friend. And he didn't want to lose the feeling that he belonged.

He changed the subject, and as soon as the first question came out, he realized he had a million more behind it. "Kai, do you live in that cottage I found you in?" he asked. "Are your parents there too? Do you live in this land as much as you live in our world? Where did the mirror come from? When you said you were waiting for me, how did you know I'd come? How are we going to get back—"

Kai laughed loudly and said, "Whoa, whoa, whoa. One thing at a time. But the most important thing first: we may have to go back suddenly. We don't know how much time we have here. Or . . ." Kai looked toward the mountain. His voice got sadder. "Or you might stay here forever. There are some things we don't have control over."

Peter said, "Wait, what? Stay here forever? What do you mean, we might have to go back suddenly?"

Kai said, "Let's worry about that later." Then he nudged his horse and went farther up the road, past Lithliel. All three horses started trotting— not Peter's favorite thing.

The rhythm of the trot made Peter stop talking. Every step was jarring, and he suddenly felt out of sorts. There were too many unanswered questions. Some pretty big questions he realized he should have asked much earlier.

Another roar shook the ground, but this time it felt much closer. Peter had to put his hands over his ears. When it was over, Lithliel looked back grimly at Peter and Kai. "We're close. Be prepared," she said, and then faced front again.

Peter put the questions out of his mind. He'd think about them after the dragon was defeated. Or whatever it was he had to do. If the witch was supposed to give him confidence, she'd failed. Peter just felt confused about everything now.

The horses had moved off the grassy plains and had started up a steep, rocky path. They'd reached the mountain. Peter looked all the way up—the mountain stretched into the clouds. The land was barren except for rocks and gray, ashy dirt. And way up the path, Peter could see a large plateau, with what looked like a huge cave. He thought he saw smoke puff out from the cave.

Peter said, "So, I guess we found the dragon, huh?"

Lithliel got off her horse. "We'll need to walk

from here. It's too steep and rocky for the horses."

Peter got off Samson and stood nervously. He patted Samson and leaned into him. He didn't want Samson to go. "Where will we tie them up?"

Lithliel said, "Hiyah!" and smacked her horse on the rump. The horse ran down the hill to the prairie, where it stopped and looked at her. Then it started eating grass. Lithliel grinned. "This is like heaven for horses. I'm pretty sure they'll stay here."

Kai got off his horse and smacked its rump too. The horse took off and stood by Lithliel's.

"Bye, Samson. Please don't leave the grass. I want to see you when I come back." Peter went to smack Samson on the rump, but the horse gave him a look and then trotted primly to the other two horses, where he immediately started eating.

Peter giggled. He giggled a little too long—

nerves made him just a little hysterical. Finally, he managed to stop himself—Kai and Lithliel were staring at him in confusion.

"Uh, should we go?" he asked, if only to get them to stop staring.

Kai grinned. "Oh, yeah." He looked way too excited to be facing a huge, menacing dragon. He turned around and started climbing. Lithliel followed him, and Peter brought up the rear.

The path got steeper and steeper. And the rocks got rockier. More than once, Peter slipped and skidded a little way down. Lithliel and Kai did too, and at one point, Peter was pretty sure all three of them were going to skid down the mountain. But they managed to find enough footholds to climb to the plateau. When they reached the edge, Kai and Lithliel climbed around the ledge of the plateau and held on, peeking their heads above the edge to view the cave. Peter joined them, trying hard not to look down. The edge of the plateau hung in space. And although there were good footholds, they weren't incredibly big, and suddenly Peter missed the security of the rocky path.

Kai whispered, "She seems to be sleeping now. Maybe we didn't need the witch's powder after all."

Sure enough, the puffs of smoke Peter had seen earlier were accompanied by a soft snore. Something about that snore made Peter feel fond of the dragon. There was something so human about snoring. He heard murmurs, too, and real- ized the dragon was talking in her sleep.

"So, Lithliel, you sneak in and throw this

sleeping powder, and then Peter and I will come in and pierce her heart." Kai looked at them. Lithliel hesitated but nodded. Peter knew this was probably hard for her—as a warrior, she probably always did the piercing.

Peter also didn't feel good about this plan. It seemed so . . . *mean.* . . .

He cleared his throat and tried to find his voice. "Um, well . . . ," he started. "If . . . why don't . . ." He stopped in frustration. No wonder Olive talked for him all the time! He couldn't find words ever! He shook his head and tried again. "Mariel said we could try to, I don't know, talk her out of being a dragon or something?" The minute he said it, he felt silly. Had she really said that? It didn't help that both Kai and Lithliel were giving him disapproving looks.

"I don't know what she meant," Lithliel said. "That seems too dangerous. I vote we go right for the heart."

Kai nodded. "I agree." Both of them looked at Peter expectantly. He sighed. Something in him just couldn't agree. There seemed to be something wrong with putting a creature to sleep and then killing it. Peter didn't want to kill anything.

"I just think we should try something besides killing her, is all," he said.

"Like what?" Kai whispered impatiently.

Peter was at a loss. "I guess talking to her?"

A voice above them boomed, "And just what would you have to say?" Peter looked up. Right into the gigantic eye of the dragon. He heard Kai and Lithliel yell as they got swept up in one of the dragon's huge claws. And he felt himself lifted up in the dragon's other claw. He, Kai, and Lithliel soared up higher than Peter would have thought possible. Now the ground was far below.

The dragon held them like toys. Her voice boomed. Something about her eyes and her voice was familiar. But Peter couldn't place it.

And anyway, there were other things to think about at that exact moment.

"Pardon me for interrupting your plans to kill me. Now tell me, brave ones. Just what would ever stop me from eating you right now?" the dragon said, smiling and showing teeth as big as Peter was tall.

For the millionth time in his life, Peter couldn't think of one thing to say.

CHAPTER 11

A Choice

Peter watched as Kai struggled to get to his pocket. Lithliel seemed to be in pain, squashed up against Kai. Peter had to act quickly. He found his voice and tried to keep the tremor from it.

"Uh, Ms. Dragon, we have a deal for you. If you could so kindly put us down, we'll talk about your, um"—he searched for the word Kai had used—"tributes."

The dragon blinked and then made a sound that Peter assumed must be dragon laughter. It rumbled all through her body. She said, "All right . . . I guess we can talk about the tributes. Will the elves make the deadline? Or will I have to ravage the entire land?"

The wind whooshed past Peter's ears as the dragon set him down. Kai and Lithliel reached the ground at the same time, and Peter saw Kai reach into his pocket, a fierce look on his face.

Peter caught Kai's glance and gave a little head shake. Kai frowned. Peter tried to communicate everything with his eyes: "Just wait. I might be able to do this."

Even the thought made him shiver. But this dragon seemed to be listening to him. He had to try another way. He felt it deep down, just like Mariel had said.

Kai gave him a disapproving look but stopped moving. He kept his hand near his pocket, though.

"Well?" said the dragon, exhaling hard. So hard it almost knocked them all back. Peter was suddenly aware of how little he was compared to the dragon. This seemed like a fool's errand—he was going to talk a dragon out of eating people? Most of the time he could barely talk at all!

He thought of Olive—she would normally jump in right about now. She used to say what was on his mind so that he wouldn't have to. That had been really annoying. But now that the focus was all on him, he found himself desperately wishing she was right there beside him.

Not to mention, the dragon could snap him up in her jaws at any moment. The thought made Peter weak in the knees.

What had Mariel said? Listen to his heart? Right now his heart was beating a million miles a minute. He took a deep breath. Then another. Then he closed his eyes and tried to slow his heartbeat down. He felt the stillness he'd felt at Mariel's house take over.

And he heard.

He heard a quiet voice telling him that the dragon was lonely. And he saw things, too. He saw a woman—a witch—who had been driven out of a village. She had just been trying to help—she'd offered her services and her magic, but no one seemed to understand. He saw flames and angry faces. And a scared, lonely, good elf-witch driven to sadness because she was so misunderstood. That sadness had turned to rage and had grown inside her. Until finally, the loneliness and sadness had burst out. And she had become a dragon.

She'd just been trying to help.

Peter felt a tear slide down his cheek. The dragon was so much more than a dragon.

He opened his eyes. "I . . . uh," he started. He swallowed and took another breath. He let the stillness come over him. When he started again, his voice was strong. "I know who you are," he said.

The dragon scoffed. "I highly doubt that, boy. What could you possibly know? Who do you think you are?"

Kai said angrily, "What right do you have to question us, Dragon? We're not the evil ones here!"

But Peter shook his head at Kai. He stepped forward. "I'm Peter. And I have something to say."

The dragon started rumbling. "Why should I listen to you?" she said, her voice getting louder and louder. Peter had the urge to cover his ears again, but he resisted.

He said simply, "Because I am listening to you."

The dragon blinked.

"I know you were turned away by your village. And I'm so sorry about that. I know how hard that must be. See, I just . . . I just moved. And I love my new friends, but I don't know where I fit. And my sister . . . she always . . . Never mind. It's not the same, I know. But I feel lonely too and like I don't belong." He wasn't quite sure where to go from there. But he could tell that the dragon was listening to him. He felt her leaning in, her great big eyes trained on him.

He realized that the best thing he could do right now was to actually stop talking and . . . listen. Something he used to be really good at. "What happened with you?" he asked quietly.

The dragon blinked and then exhaled, more slowly this time. She lay down so that her claws were outstretched, enclosing the three of them in a half-circle. Lithliel looked fascinated. She stared at Peter with wide eyes and the beginning of a smile. Kai still looked angry, for some reason. But Peter focused his attention back on the dragon.

Her voice sounded smaller. "I was a healer in a village, years and years ago. So many years I can't remember. A little girl came to me with a strange cut—I tried to heal her. I used all my magic. But nothing seemed to work. I got desperate and tried many different things, going to the ends of the earth. Finally, I thought I'd found the cure. But while I was gone, something had come over the town. I don't know what it was. A sickness. A sickness that resisted any healing. A sickness of the soul. And one by one, the villagers turned on me. These were my friends, you see. My family. When witches adopt a village, they adopt everyone in it. They become her family, and she cares for them as for her own children."

A huge tear traveled down the dragon's cheek. "It broke my heart. I walked the land, sobbing, devastated. Then I got really angry. And then one day, I woke up like this. A big dragon. A really, really, hungry dragon."

Peter wiped his own eyes. "How awful," he said. "That must have been terrible for you."

The dragon didn't answer, but her body shuddered, and Peter saw more huge tears splash on the ground.

He moved closer. He knew it wasn't the best idea, but he couldn't help himself. He edged close to her head, her large eye following him the whole way. She didn't look wary anymore—just tired and sad. Peter leaned up against her face and hugged her. "I'm sorry that happened to you."

When he touched her, a vision flashed in his head. He saw her name as clear as day: Genevieve. Her name was Genevieve.

He stood back. Just as he was about to say her name out loud—let her know she was seen, and seen as she truly was—Kai yelled, "Duck, Peter!"

Peter watched in horror as Kai threw powder at the dragon. "NOOOOOO!" he yelled. And then everything happened at once. The dragon reared up, throwing Peter several feet away. He watched helplessly as Lithliel drew her sword and the dragon cried, "TRICKSTERS! How dare you! You are all the same!" Her tail flailed and knocked rocks off the entrance of the cave. Peter watched as the sleeping powder Kai had thrown took effect. And just as the dragon's head came crashing down on the ground next to Peter, a rock from the cave came crashing down on Peter.

Right on his head.

CHAPTER 12
Back in the World

P eter! Peter! Peter!" he heard, his eyes shut and his head aching. He heard a strange beeping sound in his right ear. Things felt soft all around him, and he smelled something familiar.

And then he heard a familiar voice. "He just yelled 'No,'" the voice next to him said. He realized it was Olive.

He struggled to open his eyes. After a few

seconds, one eye opened. "Where . . . ," he said, his voice sounding croaky. He opened his other eye.

Olive stood at one side of his bed, her face worried and her eyes teary. Then he saw his dad and his other dad leaning right over her. On his other side were Lizzie and Sarah. And he heard rustling farther over and saw Tabitha and Albert Garrison there too.

"I have to help the dragon," Peter said, his voice still croaky and small. But no one heard him because they'd all let out a cheer.

"He's awake!" Sarah whispered loudly. Peter had no idea how a person could whisper as loudly as she could. Her whisper was actually louder than his normal voice.

His dads hugged each other, and Olive laid her head on his shoulder. He felt her grab his hand, but his fingertips seemed numb. He flexed his hands.

Where was he? He finally looked around the room. He was in a hospital bed, and the beeping sound was a heart monitor. He was covered in blankets, and his head felt like it was stuffed with bandages.

"I have to get back to the cottage," he said. He must somehow have disappeared into his own world again, after the rock hit him. He needed to make sure that Kai and Lithliel didn't hurt Genevieve.

Peter started to sit up, but his dad John said, "Whoa, whoa, whoa. Not so fast, buddy.

You've had quite a bump on your head and a bit of a night."

"I know. The rock hit me. But I feel okay, and I have to get back to the dragon so I can say her name," Peter said, trying to sit up again. His other dad gently put a hand on him.

Olive said, "What the heck are you talking about?"

Sarah whispered loudly to Lizzie, "I think he's broken." Lizzie shushed her.

"I . . ." He looked at everyone staring at him. He wondered if they knew where he'd been. "I was in a different land, through the mirror. And Kai and Lithliel—who looked like you, Sarah—and I had to go fight a dragon. Only I didn't want to fight it because I knew its name because of the witch, who looked like you, Lizzie . . ." His voice trailed off as he saw everyone's expression. Their expressions were saying, "You. Are. Nuts."

He cleared his throat. Maybe if he asked them what they knew . . . "What happened here?" he asked.

Albert stood up, wringing his hands. "It was all my fault, Peter," he said.

Immediately, John and David said, "No, no, no . . . ," but before anything else could happen, Sheriff Hadley and Ms. Shirvani walked in. She squealed and the sheriff said, "Holy wow, he's awake!" He was holding something that smelled like hot chocolate. Peter's stomach rumbled.

"Peter just asked what happened," Tabitha said. "And Albert was saying it was his fault—" But the sheriff jumped in.

149

"Albert, I've said it a million times. That dang dog lost her head and it was all MY fault—" Sheriff Hadley started.

But John interrupted firmly. "It was NO ONE's fault. Things like this happen. And our darling Peter is okay. Our Peter, who braved hours out there."

Peter said, "Hours out where?" He thought maybe they somehow knew about Tiar.

But Ms. Shirvani said, "Here's what happened, honey. The dog took off—ran all the way back to my apartment. Sebastian was spooked and tore off with you. It seems a branch hit you on your noggin and knocked you off the sleigh. Sebastian ran off into the forest. And you made your way to the crook of a tree and lost consciousness."

No one spoke for a moment. Peter saw Olive

crying near him, and he gave her a puzzled look. "You could have died, Peter," she said, tears streaming down her face.

Peter shook his head, but the movement hurt. All he could muster was "I'm okay." How could he let her know that he had found the cottage and that his greatest danger had come from almost being eaten by a dragon?

David wiped his eyes. "You'll never guess how we found you," he said. "It was almost magical."

John said, "The horse, Sebastian. We'd been in the woods, trying to find you, but the tracks had been covered by the snow. We were yelling and yelling. And then all of a sudden, Sebastian appeared. He'd somehow knocked the harness off and wasn't pulling the sleigh anymore. He saw us, and we followed him into the forest. He'd go a little way ahead while we followed, until we got to you. Then he stood by you and waited."

Peter smiled. "Yes, Samson is a good horse. I rode him," he said.

"No, it's Sebastian, honey," Tabitha said gently.

"What's wrong with him?" Sarah asked loudly.

Peter huffed in frustration. "That's not how it happened."

No one said anything for a second. Then Lizzie said, "How did it happen, Peter?"

But even her tone irritated him. He wasn't crazy. The whole thing HAD happened. He had almost saved the dragon—and she was still in danger. He had to find Kai.

"I . . . ," he started. "I found a cottage, and then I saw Kai from school there and we went through . . . a . . . we went through a . . ." He stopped. He realized everything he was going to say after that WOULD sound crazy. He sank back in the bed, disappointed.

All of it had felt so real. It had been real, hadn't it?

Suddenly he felt like crying. Olive looked at him and said, "I think he's tired." The adults nodded, and Lizzie gave him a sympathetic look. He looked away from her.

Olive whispered, "Do you want everyone to leave?"

At least she still sort of knew him. He nodded. Olive looked at their dads, and they got the picture.

"Why don't we all give Peter some rest? I bet he's exhausted." John leaned over and kissed Peter on the cheek. David followed and put his hand on Peter's cheek, his eyes crinkled and worried. Peter didn't want to be fawned over. He moved his cheek away.

He'd gone from someone who could save an entire land to an invalid in minutes. This was not what he wanted.

One by one, they filed out of his room. Olive lingered a little and mouthed, "Are you okay?" Peter swallowed and nodded.

Part of him wanted her to stay. He didn't want to feel alone right at that moment. But

another part of him knew she'd never understand.

As they all left, Peter felt like he knew exactly
how Genevieve felt. He let the tears fall down his
cheeks and tried to get the feeling back from the
land where he had almost been a hero.

CHAPTER 13

A Real Pain

The doctor told Peter he could go home, and that he could even go to school the following Monday. It was Thursday, so the wait was excruciating. Peter wanted to see Kai right away. Because of the accident, his dads had gotten him his own cell phone, but he didn't even have Kai's number. So on Sunday night, when his dad David said, "Maybe you should stay home just a couple more days?" Peter thought he might scream.

He saw his other dad, John, give David a glance. It looked like they had already had this conversation.

Peter felt the much smaller bandage on his head. He wasn't looking forward to any attention at school, but he desperately wanted to see Kai.

Olive looked up from her reading to say, "Peter needs to go to school. He's getting antsy and cranky." The she went back to reading her book.

He frowned. There she was, talking for him again.

Even if she was right.

"I'm FINE," he said, his voice louder than he meant it to be. Everyone looked at him in surprise.

Having everyone's attention made Peter's face burn. But . . . it also made him feel . . .

powerful. Like in Tiar, when the dragon had listened to him. And Kai had mostly listened to him. He'd almost saved a dragon and an entire world, after all.

He said, "I'm going to school tomorrow," and got up from his chair. It was family reading time, but Peter was done. He was going to storm out, but the hurt look on his dad David's face made him soften things just a little. "I'm tired. I'm going to sleep."

David got up and gave him a hug. He put his hands on Peter's cheeks and said, "My darling boy. I was so worried about you. Get some sleep."

Olive said, "Yeah, try to wake up less cranky!"

Peter narrowed his eyes at her, and she narrowed her eyes at him. But Peter saw something behind that. There was hurt there. She masked it by crossing her eyes at him, which made him smile. He crossed his eyes back, and then she made a funny face. It was a face that always made him laugh. This felt good. This felt like the old Peter and Olive.

Except the old Peter and Olive meant that Peter never got to talk. And after Tiar . . . well, he didn't think he could go back to the way it had been. He gave her a polite smile and went to his room, trying to stifle any guilt he felt.

After doing all his pre-bed routines, Peter collapsed into bed and stared through his skylight. He could see the stars—one of the coolest things about coming out to the country. He wondered if the land he'd been to was somewhere, somehow, in those stars.

He closed his eyes. He was going to see Kai

tomorrow. At least someone would know what really happened. A new friend—someone to literally go on adventures with. He drifted off to sleep with a smile on his face.

At his locker the next day, Peter craned his neck, looking everywhere for Kai. Olive groaned. "All you do is look somewhere else lately. Who are you looking for?"

"No one," Peter mumbled.

Olive grabbed some books and pushed them into his stomach. He took them without looking, still straining to see down the hall. She closed the locker and snapped her fingers in front of his face. "Hey!" she said.

"What?" he said, his voice sounding sort of mean even to his own ears.

Olive's face made him turn his full attention to her. She looked hurt—like, really hurt. She said to him, "What's happening with you?"

Peter swallowed. He hated seeing her upset. This was the second time in two days something he'd said or done had made her feel bad. Maybe if he told her some things, she might understand. She always had—she was his twin. They knew each other better than anyone. They had always been each other's best friends. At least, they used to be.

He was about to say something when there was a commotion at the end of the hall. Kai was laughing hard at something. Peter smiled too, even though he had no idea what Kai was laughing at, and even though there was no way Kai could see him.

"I gotta go," Peter said to Olive. He caught the look of disappointment on her face, but he ignored it. He had to talk to Kai. Had to talk to someone who understood him and listened to him.

He saw Kai laughing with some friends and noticed a kid whose books had spilled all over the floor. If Peter didn't know better, he'd think Kai was laughing at the kid. But that seemed unlikely. After all, Peter didn't agree with Kai's methods with the dragon, but Kai had gone there to save a world. That meant something. The kid picked up all his books before Peter got there, and then the first bell rang. Kai and Peter had language arts, so Peter followed Kai and got to his seat just seconds after him. Today Kai had decided to sit in a desk right next to Peter. The kid who normally sat there came in, furrowed his eyebrows, and sat behind Kai. Peter couldn't wait to ask Kai some questions.

The girl sitting in front of Peter said, "Whoa, what happened to you?" She pointed to his bandage. He put his hand up self-consciously. He'd forgotten it was there.

"Um . . . ," he said.

Then Kai's voice piped up. "You have no idea how he got that. And you wouldn't believe him if he told you." He looked straight at Peter, then winked. "Right?" he asked, his voice full of knowing.

Peter's heart soared.

It was real. His whole adventure had been real. HE KNEW IT.

Before he could respond, the second bell rang and Mr. Moreau breezed in. He took a look at where Kai was sitting and seemed to make a note of it. The class didn't have assigned seats— but most kids always sat in the same place. Not Kai. And Mr. Moreau always seemed to keep an eye on him.

Mr. Moreau began talking, and Peter gathered his nerve. He couldn't wait; he had to ask Kai now. He whispered to Kai, "So . . . you know the land in *Elf Mirror*?"

Kai grinned. "You know I do."

Peter grinned back. He did. He did know Tiar well.

"What happened with the dragon?" Peter asked.

Before Kai could respond, Mr. Moreau said, "Peter. I'm talking now; you can talk later."

Peter sat back. But instead of being humiliated

that he'd gotten into trouble, he felt angry. He had to talk to Kai. And even though talking back wasn't like him at all, he decided to talk back. "I'm not done, though. I still have things to say," he said.

Kai snickered. Peter looked at him, and Kai gave him a thumbs-up. Peter grinned. That thumbs-up must mean Kai needed to talk to Peter, too. Finally he could talk to someone about Genevieve.

"Peter . . . ," Mr. Moreau started. He had that same disappointed look that Olive had lately. "This isn't the time for you to talk."

Peter couldn't help himself. He said, "It's never the time for me to talk!"

Mr. Moreau gave him a confused look and continued with his lecture as if Peter hadn't said anything at all. Peter fumed at his desk. Kai leaned over and said, "Pssst," then passed him a note. It said, "We need to hang out and talk more about *Elf Mirror*."

Peter felt his tension release. He smiled and folded up the note and put it in his pocket. He looked at Kai and nodded.

Finally. Finally he could talk to his new friend about this world when no one else believed them. Peter had things to say.

CHAPTER 14
Hanging Out

After the bell rang to end class, Kai leaned into Peter as they walked out and said, "Hey, let's blow off school early, huh?"

Peter's stomach twisted. He'd never cut school before. But the idea of talking to Kai about Tiar was too tempting. Plus, Kai was a new friend—one he'd made on his own—and pretty much the coolest guy in school. It would be dumb for Peter to say no, right?

He nodded.

"Sweet. Okay, meet me at the front doors. Want to go to the skate park?" Kai said, chewing gum loudly.

Peter was confused. Why would they go there? He cleared his throat. "Um, how about the Garrison Orchard?" If they went to the orchard, though Peter didn't say this, and they wanted to find the cottage again, they'd be right there.

Kai's eyes lit up. "Yeah! That's a great idea. I've heard they have some awesome things to do there." He winked at Peter. Peter smiled.

They sure did. Like going to a different world to save it from a menacing dragon. Or, now, going to make sure Genevieve was okay. Peter wanted to talk to Kai about the sleeping powder, too. Like why he had thrown it at the dragon when Peter had almost broken through to her. He assumed Kai had had a good reason. Maybe if they strategized, they could find a way to make Genevieve trust them again. And then she'd turn back into a witch.

"Okay, Petey, let's meet before lunch. Then we're outta here." Kai blew a bubble and punched Peter lightly on the shoulder. "See ya later," he said.

Peter smiled widely before he could stop himself. Kai disappeared down the hall, and a cold, clammy feeling came over him. It was like the light had followed Kai and left Peter alone. But then he realized—his stomach was trying to tell him something. Something . . . bad.

There was no time to listen, though. None at all. He needed to talk about Tiar with Kai. He'd finally made a friend on his own, too, and he wasn't going to let that get away.

♡

Normally before lunch, Peter met with Lizzie and Sarah and Olive, but today he went straight from class toward the front doors. Suddenly, he wondered if he and Kai would get caught—could they really just walk out the doors?

Just as he rounded the corner to the front hallway, he saw a commotion. A small kid had fallen somehow, and his books had spilled all over the floor. It was the second time in just a few hours that that had happened. Peter wondered if there was some epidemic or something.

People helped the kid up, but Peter looked down at the floor and kept going. He made sure not to look at anyone, which might get their attention. Except he saw that Lizzie was there, trying to gather the kid's things. Which was just like Lizzie.

Peter tried to walk by without catching her eye, but just as he went to turn his head, she looked up. Her face grew quizzical, and for a second, Peter's stomach flipped. This would be a good chance to turn back. But before he could say anything, the kid started to cry loudly, and from out of nowhere Kai appeared and put his arm around Peter.

"There's a diversion, you see. So we can get out of here." He led Peter to the doors, and no one seemed to notice as they opened them. All the teachers were busy helping the kid. Peter wanted to see if Lizzie was watching, but Kai walked them out too fast.

The air was pretty warm for winter when they got outside—nothing like the night Peter had been knocked unconscious. They hurried from the school and turned down the road. It seemed they'd gotten away with it and that no one was following them. Still, it was a pretty long walk to the orchard. Peter wished he'd thought a little more about the plan.

"Dude, don't worry! You look so worried," Kai said. "My older brother is going to give us a ride. I texted him. We just need to get to the end of the road."

Peter cleared his throat. "How old is your brother?" he asked.

Kai said, "Seventeen," as he typed on his phone. Suddenly, something occurred to Peter.

His new phone. He pulled it out of his pocket, and there was a text from Lizzie: Is everything okay?

He knew that meant, "Where were you going?"

But worse, he knew that his dads or Olive could track him on the tracking app they all had.

He chewed his lip and thought about it.

He made a decision. "Uh, hold on," he said to Kai. Peter ran as fast as he could back to the school, ducking to make sure no one would see him. His heart pounded wildly—he felt just like he had when he'd faced Genevieve. He stuffed his cell phone into his backpack and tossed the pack to the side of the school. Then he turned around and sprinted back to Kai as fast as he could.

It wasn't that far, but Peter was winded. Being scared took his breath away.

Kai laughed. "DUDE! That was awesome! You could have gotten caught. You're crazy. I think we're going to make a great team!" He grabbed Peter's arm and said, "Come on, my brother's here. We need to make it down the road."

They ran the rest of the way to the intersection,

where a beat-up car sat, idling. A boy who looked a lot like Kai sat in the car, smoking. "Get in, loser," the guy said. Kai got in the front and punched his brother hard. "You're a loser," he said.

Peter hesitated. This was a strange person's car, and he was smoking. Kai said, "Come on, Petey. We have to get going. Petey here is wild, Ander. We're going to have a good time today." "Whatever," the kid said, flipping the cigarette out of the car window. Peter frowned but got in. This suddenly didn't seem so fun.

Something occurred to Peter. "Um, shouldn't you be in school?" he asked Ander.

Ander looked at Kai. "Petey doesn't sound that crazy, Kai."

Kai turned around and looked at Peter, a frown on his face. It looked so much like the frown of the Kai from Tiar who was disappointed in Peter talking to the dragon. For a minute, Peter felt woozy. He swallowed.

He needed to make this right. "Just a joke, man," he said, in a voice he hardly recognized.

Ander snickered.

The rest of the short ride was pretty quiet, but Peter felt relieved when they got to the orchard. Luckily, no one was around. The Garrisons must have been in town getting things for the solstice celebration coming up. When Peter and Kai got out of the car, a cold wind whipped through Peter's hair. Suddenly, things seemed a little ominous.

Ander shot off without a word, and Kai watched the car retreat. "My brother's so cool," he said, almost to himself.

Peter disagreed. But he knew that probably wasn't a smart thing to say.

Instead, he said, "Um, can I show you something? Do you want to follow me?"

Kai clapped his arm around Peter's shoulders. "Sure, Petey! This place was your idea. You got an interesting world to show me or something?" He grinned at Peter, and finally, Peter's stomach settled down a little. Though he wished Kai would just come out and say the word, "Tiar." It made Peter nervous that he wouldn't just say the name of the world. Which made Peter not want to say it either. Maybe there was a reason Kai wasn't talking about it?

"Okay, let's go," Peter said, trudging through the snow. He had to stop himself from running.

Soon they were at the barn. Peter heard the horses snorting in their stalls.

This would surely allow Kai and Peter to talk about Tiar. And more: maybe he and Kai could find a way back together. Maybe see if the Garrisons would let them ride horses on their own soon. They could go look for the cottage together.

At the sight of the barn, Kai stopped and frowned. "You're showing me horses?" he said to Peter, his eyebrows furrowed.

Suddenly, Peter felt silly. He stammered, "Uh . . . I—I thought you . . . maybe . . ." But then Kai roared with laughter.

"You're too easy to tease, man. This is awesome! Horses just like *Elf Mirror*. Only real!" He grinned.

Peter's heart soared. Finally, they could talk about getting back to Tiar, and make a plan to save Genevieve and the world.

CHAPTER 15

Wild Horses

Sweet! I can't wait to ride one!" Kai said as he walked to the barn. "I mean, I've never ridden one before, but it can't be that hard, right?" He winked at Peter.

But now Peter was confused. Was Kai kidding? That nervous feeling in his stomach was back. He felt like he was on a roller coaster. One second he thought Kai and he were on the same page, and the next it felt like they weren't even reading the same book.

He frowned, looking down at the ground. He needed to just come out and say it.

He swallowed and listened to their feet crunching in the snow. They reached the barn doors before Peter could say the words. But he finally did. "Well, in the *Elf Mirror* world—Tiar— you were pretty good," he said.

Kai looked on the doors for a latch. He said, "Oh, well, that's just a game. Is that the name of the world in *Elf Mirror*? I didn't know. Man, you're totally into it. We should play it sometime."

Peter's heart beat hard in his chest. "Don't you . . . remember when we . . ." He felt like he was going to cry. "Have you been to the cottage in the forest?" he asked, his voice higher than he wanted it to be.

Kai paused and looked at him. "Dude, this is the first time I've been here. I don't know what you're talking about." Then his eyes lit up. "Aha!"

He undid the latch on the barn doors, and before Peter could get his bearings, he had slid them open. "Wow. They didn't even lock this. The people who live here are idiots."

Peter shook his head to snap out of it. "No . . . ," he started, but Kai was walking along the horses' stalls, running his hands along the wood and rapping on it occasionally. Each time he did that, the horses snorted and startled, and Kai laughed.

He stopped at a stall that held a large, beautiful brown horse with a dark muzzle and a white diamond on her forehead.

"This one!" he said, and began to open the stall door.

Peter took a deep breath and tried to push the hurt aside. Finally, everything came into focus and he realized three things: there was no "real" world that they had gone to; he had hit his head and just had a vivid dream; and Kai was no hero.

And he was stealing a horse.

Peter watched helplessly as Kai used the stall door to get on the horse, which was shifting nervously in the stall. Kai was going to ride her bareback. And he'd never ridden before. Peter sprang into action.

"Kai!" he yelled, just as Kai swung his leg up. "Kai, wait! Don't do that. You need someone to help you." Peter started sweating under his winter cap. The smell of hay and horse suddenly seemed overwhelming to him. "Let's just go ask the Garrisons if they can help us."

As he said that, Kai thwumped onto the horse's back, and the horse whinnied. Peter cringed. He needed to find a way to get through to Kai. He felt a little bit like he was talking to the dragon again.

Kai laughed. "Oh, come on, Petey, what can this hurt? How hard can this be?"

Peter didn't even know where to start.

Kai wrapped his hands in the horse's mane. "Okay, in movies I know you kick the horse to get it started, right?"

Peter watched as Kai, seemingly almost in slow motion, raised his legs and then lowered them back down, kicking the horse. Peter yelled, "NOOOO!"

But it was too late. The horse shot out of the

barn, with Kai barely hanging on. When the horse got to the fence, she jumped and sent Kai flying.

In that short time, the horse and Kai had gotten far enough for Peter to have to run to where Kai had fallen.

As he ran, he watched the horse take off down the path to the forest. And then disappear into the trees.

Peter finally caught up to Kai, who had started to sit up in the snow. At first he thought Kai was crying, but then he realized he was laughing.

Peter slid to his knees next to him. "Are you okay?" he asked, looking for any bumps or limbs at weird angles.

But Kai just laughed. "That was AWESOME," he said. "I can't wait to tell my brother about this!" He bounded back up, brushing snow off his coat.

Peter looked up at him for a second in disbelief. Finally, he stood up.

"You . . . you stole a horse. And now it's gone," Peter said, his voice cracking a little.

Kai said, "Petey, this was a great idea! What should we do next?"

Peter shook his head. "We have to find that horse. I know the people who live here. . . ."

"Don't they have farmhands or whatever here?" Kai asked, looking around the orchard. "They'll just blame it on one of them or something." He frowned. "There isn't that much out here, huh? I guess this was the only thing to do." He took out his phone and started texting. "No worries. My brother is in trouble and part of his punishment is having to take me where I want to go. I'll have him come pick us up."

Peter looked helplessly out to the forest. How would they ever get that horse back? And he didn't want someone else to get in trouble for what they had done.

He would be in so much trouble if he told someone what had happened. His stomach felt like it had been punched.

Kai finished texting and then saw the look on Peter's face. "Hey, dude, it's okay. Horses find their way back. They're like dogs. I read about this," he said.

Peter saw Ander's car pull up by the entrance to the orchard. Everything was happening too fast. Peter couldn't think.

Kai grinned. "He must not have gone very far." He put his arm around Peter again and pulled him toward the car. "What a great adventure, huh? Seriously, dude, that horse will come back. They always do. But we should get out of here before someone finds out, right? And let's make sure not to tell anyone. It'll be our secret."

The voice inside Peter definitely disagreed. But Peter tamped it down and pretended that it would be okay.

CHAPTER 16

Listen

Everything was not okay.

When Peter got into the car with Ander and Kai, everything felt awful. After riding for just a few minutes, he asked to be let out.

Ander said, "What's with this kid?"

And Kai shrugged. "Guess he doesn't know how to have fun."

Peter shut the door without looking at either

of them and walked the mile or so home. He felt numb. Heavy. And like nothing in the world would ever be right again.

When he got home, his dad David was sitting in the living room, his cell phone pressed to his ear. When he saw Peter, he said, "Oh, thank God. He's here." Olive was sitting next to him, her face stricken. When Peter walked in, she jumped off the couch and ran over to him. She threw her arms around his neck.

"We thought you were hurt or kidnapped or something!" she yelled into his neck.

He felt other arms around him—dad arms. He felt like crying. Did he even deserve this sort of homecoming after what he'd done? He disentangled himself and looked at the floor.

"I'm sorry," he whispered, barely able to talk at all.

"Peter. What happened? Did you . . . cut school?" David asked, his voice rising in surprise. Cutting school was so very unlike Peter.

Peter nodded and kept looking at the floor. Olive backed up a little. "Why, Peter?"

He shrugged. The tears were going to come any minute now. "Can I go to my room?" he asked, his voice low and choked.

David was quiet for a moment. "Yes. You need to go to your room. And when John gets home, we'll decide your punishment. But for now, no video games. And no phone, since you can't seem to take care of it." He pointed to the couch. "Luckily, Olive found your backpack."

Peter bit his lip and turned around. When he got to the bottom of the stairs, his dad said words that broke Peter's heart. "I'm so disappointed in you, Peter."

The tears fell and Peter ran up the stairs.

He knew the feeling.

He didn't come down for dinner, and he barely slept. So when Olive came to his room in the morning, he was hungry and tired. But mostly he still felt awful and like nothing in the world was right.

Olive hovered near the door. "Can I come in?" she asked. She never asked. Something about her asking made him sadder. He shrugged.

She came in and sat on his bed while he

looked for his shoes. He still couldn't look Olive in the eye.

"Peter."

He turned around slowly, frowning.

"What's going on?" He saw tears in her eyes. "Why . . . ?" she started, and then took a deep breath. To Peter's surprise, it seemed like she couldn't find words. This never happened to Olive.

She pushed her glasses up her nose, sniffed, and then said, "Peter, why won't you talk to me anymore?"

Peter really looked at her for the first time since she'd entered his room. His eyes, too, sprang tears. He wanted to say something. But all his feelings were just a big ball of confusion. And how could he tell her what he'd done the night before? To their new best friend?

He looked down and then up again. "I don't know" was all he said. His voice cracked.

Olive's shoulders sagged and she nodded. She got up and walked to the door. Then she turned around and said, "You know, you're always my best friend, no matter what. Best friends always." Then she left.

For the second time in twenty-four hours, Peter cried.

Because of Peter's antics, his dads had decided they would drive Olive and Peter to school, even though the weather was pretty nice. By the time they were all loaded in the car, Peter had gotten control of himself. To his relief, Olive and his dads talked the whole time. But once they were at school, Peter's stomach clenched.

He was going to see Kai. He had no idea what to say to him.

But instead of finding Kai when he walked down the hall, he saw Lizzie by her locker. She looked like she had been crying. Sarah appeared near her and handed her something. By the time Peter got there, he could see it was a Kleenex.

Peter got to his locker and stood there awkwardly. "Um, are you okay?" he asked, afraid of the answer. He had a sinking feeling he knew why Lizzie was crying.

Lizzie turned to him, her eyes red and puffy. She shook her head. "I'm just worried, that's all. It's so cold. And someone let my horse, Star, out of the barn. We can't figure out who. I'm just so worried she's hurt!"

Olive arrived next and put her arms around Lizzie's neck. "I saw your texts last night. I'm so sorry."

Sarah's face darkened. "I'd love to get my hands on the jerk who did this. You'd have to be a terrible, terrible person to do something like this."

Lizzie burst into tears again, and Peter felt like he was going to pass out. This was all his fault. The horse hadn't come back—of course she hadn't. He had known that yesterday, some-where deep inside, but he hadn't listened to himself. He'd done the opposite of what he'd learned in Tiar.

Whether or not that world was real, he'd learned some things. And he'd ignored them all, thinking the important part was his friendship with Kai.

As if Peter had conjured him up with a magic spell, Kai walked down the hallway. He stopped next to Peter.

Peter swallowed. Kai looked at Lizzie and said, "What's happening? You making girls cry, Petey?"

Olive scrunched her face, making her glasses ride up her nose. Peter could practically hear her thought: "He calls you Petey?"

Sarah glared at him. "No. Some jerk let out her favorite horse, and we're afraid it's lost or hurt."

Kai snorted. "She's crying about that? What a baby. Or are you so sad because that horse was your boyfriend?" He guffawed at his own joke and put his arm around Peter. "Come on, Petey. We've got things to do."

But suddenly Peter saw everything clearly. Even in Tiar, Kai hadn't been very nice. Peter had known that, too—he'd just ignored it and had seen what he wanted to see. Kai had wanted to kill the dragon because he wanted an adventure. Because he wanted to be seen as a hero. But really, he was the exact opposite. Peter had known it all along.

Peter felt the voice inside him welling up and getting louder. He looked at one of his best friends crying, and his sister—best friend always—looking at him like she didn't even know him.

This wasn't who he was. He needed to listen

to that voice inside him, just like Mariel had said. It knew what to do.

And then Peter knew what to do.

He stepped away from Kai. "NO!" he said loudly. He felt the anger rise in him, and suddenly the words wouldn't be bottled up. "You do not talk to people like that. You do not talk to my friend like that! Go away!" Peter was shaking, and he realized he'd yelled all this in the hallway. Several kids had stopped and were staring. Normally, this would be mortifying to Peter. But today he didn't care. This had to be said.

Kai stared at him in disbelief. "Why are you freaking out? It was just a joke. We're friends, dude."

Peter stood tall. He walked up close to Kai

and said, "You are not my friend. And you need to leave my *actual* friends alone." Then he backed up and stood in front of Lizzie. He felt Olive and Sarah flank him. So now there were three people in front of Lizzie, all mad as hornets.

Peter felt right at home.

Kai said, "Whatever. It's not like you're an angel, PETEY. Why don't you tell your friend here what you did? I'm out of here." And he walked away in a huff.

For the first time in a long while, Peter felt his stomach unclench. He finally felt like he was doing the right thing, being who he was on the inside. He had listened to the voice in his heart and had spoken it out loud. And it felt good.

The girls crowded around him and hugged

him, Olive squeezing the tightest. Peter hugged back, but he still wasn't totally happy.

There was something he had to do to truly make everything right. He'd just have to wait until he got a minute alone.

CHAPTER 17
Saving the Day

When Peter got home from school, he yelled something at his dads and Olive about needing some time alone, and he shut his door. He'd barely been able to think of anything else during school, and now that he was home, he hurried up with his plan. He grabbed his backpack and filled it with a bottle of water, his phone, a snack, and a first aid kit.

Then he did something he'd never done

before: he snuck out his window.

It wasn't hard. There was a giant old oak right by his window, and when they'd first moved in, his dads had even joked about him sneaking out.

Sometimes parents were right about things.

Peter sprinted down the road, breathing hard and readjusting his backpack every few steps. This was a pretty impulsive thing to do. And he was sure he'd be in trouble for sneaking out, of course. But now that he'd really listened to his inside voice, he couldn't get it to stop talking.

And it said, "Find Lizzie's horse."

He had caused this mess, and he would fix it. He just hoped he could do it before it got dark out. And he wanted to do it before he told everyone what he'd done. Maybe that would make it easier to admit to.

The orchard felt farther away than ever, and he was pretty sure he would never get there. When he finally did, he was sweaty and out of breath, and also incredibly cold. Some of his confidence had waned, but he was still determined.

He walked up to the barn and heard people talking. He ran to the barn wall and stood up against it, hoping no one would see him. He heard Sheriff Hadley and Albert inside the doors. He couldn't hear what they were saying, but he peeked around the corner. They walked to the far end of the barn where the other doors were and disappeared. Peter took a deep breath and snuck inside. He walked along the stalls. He saw the stall where Star had been, still empty. And then he spotted Sebastian.

He set his backpack down and went up to the horse.

"Hey, Sebastian," he said, stroking the horse's head. "Do you feel like working today?" Sebastian snorted and moved his head up and down, almost like a nod. Peter smiled. Almost exactly like Samson. "Okay. I'm going to put a saddle on you and a headstall. I think I remember from horseback-riding camp how to do that. But I'm wondering if you'll take it a little easy on me? I rode a horse in Tiar, but it's been a while here. But I want to help you find your friend."

Sebastian nuzzled into Peter, and Peter hugged him. Then he went into the stall and thought back to what he'd learned about how to saddle a horse. He looked at all the equipment. A saddle pad . . . he remembered that. A saddle. Some strange straps. A brush.

A brush. He needed to brush Sebastian.

That had been his favorite part at camp. He took the brush and, too gently at first, ran it over Sebastian. But then he got the hang of it, and soon Sebastian was almost leaning into him. Peter put the brush down and looked at the rest of the equipment.

He was lost. There was no way he'd remember how to put on a saddle. And it might hurt Sebastian if he did it wrong.

He took a deep breath and said to Sebastian, "Okay, buddy. I'm going to have to ride you bareback. Remember when I asked you to be gentle?"

Flashbacks from horseback-riding camp played in his head. They'd ridden bareback more than a few times, but it was extra-scary for Peter. He closed his eyes, squared his shoulders, and opened the stall door. Then he used the wall of the stall to climb up on Sebastian's back, trying to control any fear he had.

Sebastian whinnied when Peter landed. Peter patted his neck and held on to his mane. Not so bad so far.

"Sebastian, can you take me to Star?"

The horse whinnied again and moved forward. The movement made Peter clench everything, and he remembered he had to relax to ride the horse. He remembered his instructor telling him to be relaxed but active. Whatever that meant.

He relaxed his legs, and Sebastian moved forward again. Peter held Sebastian's mane tightly and had to force himself to release his fingers just a little bit. He took a deep breath, like Mariel in Tiar had told him to do, and let himself relax all over.

He found a way to be relaxed but active. Or at least he thought so. Sebastian walked slowly out of the barn, and Peter looked left and right. He didn't see the sheriff or Albert, and he hoped it stayed that way. He had to get to the forest before they saw him, and he liked this pace.

Sebastian, as if he knew how nervous Peter was, walked slowly and deliberately. And without Peter having to tell him, he turned toward the path in the forest. When they'd reached the tree line, Peter sighed in relief. He'd made it without anyone seeing him. And he'd stayed on Sebastian. He leaned over to pat Sebastian's neck. It turned out, Peter loved riding horses. Or at least, he loved riding Sebastian. Though he was pretty sure he wasn't doing it right. It didn't matter—as long as he was still on the horse, Peter was calling it a win.

"Let's find Star, okay?" he said to Sebastian, his voice sounding loud in the quiet. Peter liked that. After a few minutes of walking, Sebastian veered off the path and into the forest. A part of the forest that Peter recognized because of the broken brush—this was where he and Sebastian had flown through. He was quiet for a moment, but then he wondered: Was Sebastian taking him to the cottage?

Peter held his breath as they moved through the trees. Sure enough, Sebastian seemed to be going the exact way they had that night. Peter could tell because of all the broken trees and the debris that looked like it had been run over by a sleigh. He was surprised that the sleigh had done that much damage. Riding in the forest was much different from riding on the path, though. Peter had to concentrate to hold on. He constantly felt like he was going to fall off. He stopped looking around and clung to Sebastian, forgetting to be relaxed but active.

Suddenly, Sebastian stopped. Peter was thrown forward a little, and he squeezed his eyes shut, but then managed to regain his balance. When he opened his eyes, he saw the tree he'd hidden from the cold in. Excitement shot through him— the cottage. This was where the cottage was! Maybe he'd been wrong and Sebastian knew that this was where the other world was. Peter looked up excitedly, but all he saw was a clearing and . . .

Star.

Sebastian had taken him to Star.

CHAPTER 18
Just Like Magic

Peter could hardly believe his eyes. Was this really happening? Star shifted and snorted a little but then walked up to Sebastian and Peter as if she had nothing better to do and was saying hi.

"Star!" Peter said. "I'm so glad you're okay!" But then Peter realized the problem. How would he get Star back to the orchard?

"Uh," Peter said to Sebastian. "Let's go back."

Since Star had come over to them, he hoped that meant she'd follow. Peter pulled Sebastian's mane and applied some pressure with his legs. Sebastian responded and turned to face the direction they'd come from, walking at the same slow pace. Peter dared to look back as he tried to hold on. Sure enough—Star was following.

Elation shot through him. He might actually be able to make things right. Just as he had the thought, he heard his name.

"PETER!" he heard, then more voices calling his name. Sebastian and Peter and Star had gotten to the path again, and now they all emerged from the trees. What Peter saw made his heart both heavy and happy. He hadn't realized so many emotions could exist at the same time.

Lizzie, Sarah, and Olive walked up the path

toward him calling his name, only about fifty feet away. Olive was in front, looking frantically along the tree line. When she spotted him, she said, "YES!"

Lizzie, Sarah, and Olive started running to him. Sebastian sidestepped nervously, so Peter shouted out, "Whoa! I'll come to you. Let's not make the horses nervous." He squeezed his legs and leaned forward, and Sebastian walked on. It wasn't long before they had reached his friends and his sister.

Lizzie ran around them and hugged Star. Her voice full of tears, she said, "You found Star! How? We looked for her everywhere last night."

Peter grinned and shrugged. "Magic, I guess."

Lizzie laughed. "Hey, Sarah, give me a boost

to get on Star." Sarah laced her fingers together at Star's side, and Olive stood on the other side to keep the horse still. Lizzie stepped into Sarah's hands and swung her leg over Star. She hugged Star hard and told her she loved her.

"I didn't know you were so good at riding horses, Peter. Riding bareback takes a lot of practice," she said.

Olive and Peter laughed at the same time. " I didn't know I was either," Peter said.

Olive looked up at him where he sat on Sebastian. "I think there are a lot of cool things we're going to find out about you," she said.

"Why are you all here? I mean, don't get me wrong—I'm glad. But how did you find me and why'd you come looking?" Peter asked.

Sarah answered, "Olive texted us and said you

probably went to the orchard to find Star. So we came too! There's no way we'd let you run out on us and get yourself into trouble. We're all best friends. We get in trouble together." She grinned at Peter and patted Sebastian.

Peter thought his heart would explode. He'd thought he didn't belong, that they didn't care about him that much. But here they were.

Sarah went on, "It must have been Olive's extra-special twin power. You know—she just KNEW where you were. That's so cool!"

Olive grinned. "Yep! It was twin power!" she said. "Or I just tracked your phone."

Peter cracked up, and so did Lizzie and Sarah. "But how did you know I was gone?" Peter asked.

Olive shrugged. "I went in to talk to you and you weren't there. And your window was open, so

I knew you snuck out. And then I did too!" Peter laughed hard at this.

Lizzie said, "You've been busy today, Peter. You snuck out, found my horse . . . and talked down a bully! I've never seen you so mad. It was kind of fun to hear you yell." She laughed a little. "Anyway, I wanted to thank you for standing up for me like that. Not that I'm surprised. I knew you would."

Her confidence in him made him teary. He looked down at the ground and gathered his courage. "Before we go back, I have to tell you something, Lizzie. You might not think I'm that great in a minute."

Lizzie rode up to him on Star, and Peter looked her in the eye. He took a deep breath and said, "It was my fault Star ran away. I came here with Kai and he tried to ride her, but she ran away. I'm so sorry."

He looked away. It had been harder to say than he'd thought. But it'd had to be done. After a beat, he heard a soft laugh. Lizzie said, "Peter. I know. I saw you leave school."

Peter looked up in surprise. Sarah said, "Wait, what?"

Lizzie shrugged. "Who else would come to the orchard in the middle of the day, right around the same time you left school? I just figured you'd tell me if you wanted to."

Peter gaped. "You're not mad at me?"

Lizzie smiled. "Nah. I figured you'd tell me eventually. It's just who you are. Plus, I knew you'd figure out pretty quick that Kai wasn't very nice. And this is a bonus! You came to find my horse and you found her! How could I be mad?"

Peter's face scrunched up, and he said, "I'm so sorry, Lizzie. And I'm sorry to all of you. I haven't been a great friend lately, I know. But things will be better now. They really will be." He'd doubted them for too long. And even knowing what a jerk he'd been, they'd showed up for him.

A person couldn't belong more than that.

They'd reached the end of the path, and Peter heard a lot of voices. At the barn, a group of people were milling around, until someone spoke on a megaphone. "Okay, people of New Amity! We are looking for Star! And, it seems, Olive and Peter? John and David have tracked their cell phones to the barn, but they aren't here, it seems? Come to think of it . . . we're probably looking for Lizzie, too."

A voice yelled out, "If Lizzie, then Sarah, too!"

"Right. So we're looking for Star, Olive, Peter, Lizzie, and Sarah. If everyone could stand in a line here—"

Then the voice said, "Oh! Good job, everyone! You found them!" The voice belonged to Albert, and as they neared, they saw him pointing at them. People turned around, and everything happened in a flash.

Peter's dads came over and helped him off Sebastian, then hugged him tightly. Tabitha and Albert corralled the horses into the barn. There was a flurry of activity and hugs, and Peter barely had a chance to think.

When he came up for air, he saw that almost the whole town of New Amity was there.

He saw Hakeem and Stella, Annabelle, Aaron

and Rachel, Sheriff Hadley . . . basically everyone he'd seen in elf version in Tiar. When his dads were done hugging him, John asked, "Did we just see you riding bareback on a horse?"

David added, "And did you find Star?"

Peter nodded, suddenly very tired. "It's a long story," he said. "But I'll tell you all of it tonight. And you can decide how long I'm grounded."

John and David both smiled. John said, "Oh, yes. We'll talk."

Peter was still confused about something. "Why is everyone here? Is there a rehearsal for the solstice or something?"

David chuckled and squeezed him. "We take care of each other in New Amity. If one of us needs help, we all help."

Peter leaned into his dad and felt warm all over. The sun had started to set, and the sky was streaked with pink and orange. When he looked up, he saw snow begin to fall.

It felt just like magic.

That night, Peter had a long talk with his dads. He told them everything and said he was sorry. His dads took away *Elf Mirror*, which made Peter incredibly happy. He didn't think he wanted to see anything that reminded him of it for a long, long time. Finally, when Peter's voice started getting hoarse, they let him go upstairs.

Peter wasn't done yet, though.

He went to Olive's room and knocked on the door. She opened it, then turned and didn't say a word. Peter knew that meant "Come in."

He walked in and sat on her bed. "I'm sorry" was all he said.

Olive sat across from him and sighed. "Why has everything been so weird with us?"

Peter looked away and gathered his thoughts. "I just . . . I started to feel like I wasn't really a part of the group. And that no one would listen to me. You and Sarah are . . ." He borrowed a phrase he'd heard his dads use: "You have strong person-alities. Sometimes it's like you don't even know I'm there. And you just talk for me sometimes."

Olive bit her lip and looked down. She started to say something but stopped herself and pushed up her glasses. "I'm listening," she said.

Peter smiled. "It seemed like you were bet-ter friends with Lizzie and Sarah and that I'm just an add-on. I started missing my old friends in Boston and then started to feel further and further away from you . . . So when I saw Kai, I thought I could make a friend on my own."

Olive nodded, and Peter went on. "But what I didn't realize is that I just misunderstood you. You were only trying to help me."

Olive sighed. "Yes. But not in the right way, I think. I should let you talk and listen to what you say."

Peter grinned. "And I should speak up."

Olive grinned back. "Okay. So it's a deal? I won't speak for you anymore, and you're going to speak up. Right?"

"RIGHT!" Peter practically yelled. Olive giggled.

He stood up, feeling lighter and better than

he had since they'd moved to New Amity. "Oh, and if you feel yourself turning into a dragon, just come talk to me, okay?"

Olive's eyebrows furrowed and she said, "What?"

Peter laughed. "Never mind. Best friends always?"

Olive smiled. "Best friends always."

That night, Peter dreamed he was in Tiar again. He was on the plateau with the dragon, but Kai wasn't there. It was Lithliel, Mariel, and him. And after he hugged the dragon, she transformed into a beautiful elf with glasses. And the four of them walked off the mountain, got onto their horses, and rode away, best friends forever.

ACKNOWLEDGMENTS

There are always too many people to thank because there are so many amazing people in this world—and I seem to know all of them. So, in no particular order:

My editor, Emma, is the most awesomest, amazingest, fantasticest editor there is. She really is. Thank you, Emma Sector, for your keen insight and encouragement. You're the best!

And of course my agent, Ammi-Joan Paquette, must always be thanked because she is brilliant, hardworking, and a tireless champion of her authors, including me. And she's also a brilliant author herself! I'm forever grateful she has let me join her team.

To my friends for their tireless support of me, including, but not at all limited to, Anne Ursu, Megan Vossler, Jenny Halstead, Natalie Harter, and Beth Brezenoff.

A huge thank-you to Sophie Kahnke, who helped me launch the first book in this series and who belongs to my forever-friend Sharon Kahnke. (Ella, you know you rocked it at the launch, right? Just wanted to mention that here.) Anyway, Sophie Kahnke—you are awesome and fantastic and please always let your light shine and be your amazing self!

Finally, always and forever a thank-you to my parents. They were and are the best parents there are. Dad, you are my rock. And Mom, I miss you always and forever and love you both so much, it hurts.

Don't miss Book 3:

A FALL FOR FRIENDSHIP

Olive doesn't believe in ghosts, but she does admit that something weird is going on at the orchard. Find out what the gang is up to in the third Orchard Novel!

ABOUT THE AUTHOR

MEGAN ATWOOD is a writer, editor, and professor in Minneapolis whose most recent books include the Dear Molly, Dear Olive series. When she's not writing books for kids of all ages, she's making new friends, going on zombie hayrides, and eating as much ice cream as she can. And, always, petting her two adorable cats, who "help" her write every book.